ALL
Because
OF YOU

ALL
Because
OF YOU

THERESA PAOLO

Dedicated to Dad

For still calling me to check that I locked the door and for being the dad who wears monster slippers.

Dear Reader,

As with all my small towns, Morgan's Bay is fictional, however I placed this town on Long Island, a place where I was born, raised and still reside. While Morgan's Bay may not be real, I've taken all of my favorite parts of the east end of Long Island and used them to create this small town.

Each book I infuse a little bit of myself and this book has many personal Easter eggs. The name Morgan's Bay came from the marina my parents kept their boat docked and where I spent many summers. Olivia's parents Yorkshire Terrier, is based on my own parents Yorkie, Frank, and who I refer to as my little brother.
And like all my other books, there will also be Easter eggs that will tie all of my small towns into one world. Keep an eye open for them while reading.

I am pleased to welcome you to Morgan's Bay.

Theresa

chapter 1

The lights were dimmed in her New York City penthouse, the champagne chilling in the ice bucket, and Olivia Green was stripped down to her newest red lace lingerie set. Her boyfriend, Daniel James III, was just selected to be included in Forbes 30 Under 30 list, and she was ready to celebrate.

She'd had plans to head home to her small town on the eastern end of Long Island to pay her parents a monthly visit, but they understood why she couldn't make it this month. At least that's what she convinced herself. The disappointment in Mom's tone wasn't exactly coinciding with her words, but Olivia had her own life now, and her parents needed to accept that.

Outside the floor-to-ceiling windows, the setting sun casted an orange glow throughout the bedroom. Olivia sprawled out on the California king, and the thousand thread Egyptian cotton rubbed softly against the exposed skin of her curves. She got into different poses and tried to find the sexiest one that showed off just enough of the red lace while still leaving a little to the imagination.

After flopping around like a fish, she finally settled on her side, elbow bent and propping her head up. She draped one leg over the other and angled her body toward the door. According to the alarm clock on her side of the bed, Daniel would be home in five minutes. The man ran on a very calculated schedule that she knew like the back of her hand.

He would come home in five minutes after having drinks with clients, change out of his suit and tie, and head into the home office to go through the emails he didn't manage to get to during the day. A little shake up in his routine was exactly what he needed. He was bestowed one of the greatest honors as an entrepreneur, and he deserved a night to celebrate.

The sun dipped lower into the horizon, and Daniel still hadn't come home. Maybe his clients bought him an extra drink. It's not like he knew she'd be home waiting for him. She thought about texting him, but her phone was in the other room, and it took her so long to get this pose down. Even if the crook of her elbow ached from being stuck in the same position, and her neck stiffened. Beauty was pain… and so was sex appeal, apparently.

They'd both been busy with work that their sex life had fizzled in the last year. It was a far cry from the days when he would take her on his desk after hours at the office when they both would stay later than necessary. She wanted that thrill again, back when she was his intern and before she became his live-in girlfriend, and tonight was the night.

If he'd ever get home…

Finally, twenty minutes later—the ice melting, the pretty sun glow gone—the door clicked open, and she perfected her pose. Anticipation swirled in her stomach, and excitement raced through her veins as she waited for him to discover his red laced vixen.

The sound of his keys dropping in the dish by the door

echoed through the apartment, followed by a loud thump. Did he walk into something? She resisted the urge to call out and ruin the surprise. She'd spent far too long planning to let it all go up in smoke because he might've banged his knee. She would make it all better as soon as he got in here.

Another thump sounded outside the bedroom, and her body shifted in curiosity. Maybe he was drunk, though, that only happened on very rare occasions. Making Forbes 30 Under 30 was a rare occasion. If he was drunk, would he even remember the picture she spent hours trying to create? She would have to make it as memorable as possible.

She lifted, allowing her nipple to peek out over the lace, and shifted forward so her breasts displayed their full potential. The door flew open, and Olivia fixed a smile on her face, but it quickly slipped to a gasp. Daniel's lips left the topless redhead in his arms whose bare legs were wrapped securely around his waist. Her skirt was pushed up over her thighs.

"Olivia!" His eyes widened, and he dropped the woman to the floor. She hit with a loud and resounding thud.

Shock and anger wagered war in Olivia's head, and she wasn't going to sit around and wait for her emotions to work it out. She jumped from the bed, grabbing the comforter and wrapping it around her practically naked body.

"You were supposed to be at your parents," Daniel choked out, like that would make this okay.

"And you weren't supposed to be tongue deep into another woman!" She pointed a furious finger at the redhead on the floor.

Tears pricked Olivia's eyes, and she wished she was strong enough to hold them back, act as if her heart wasn't breaking into a million pieces, but she was never the strong one. Tears flowed down her cheeks, dripping onto the rounded mounds of her breasts.

"How could you?" she asked.

Daniel scrubbed a hand over his face and the redhead stood, covering herself with her arm. "I'm just going to go." She hurried to the door and stopped. "Call me," she said to Daniel, and Olivia stumbled back at the audacity. By the time the shock wore off, the girl was gone.

Olivia stormed to the walk-in closet and reached for an article of clothing from one of the hundreds of hangers. There was no way she was going to have a conversation with her cheating boyfriend in nothing more than a few well-placed pieces of lace. She grabbed a dress and dropped the comforter.

On the other hand. She wanted him to see what he was missing. Six months with a highly sought-after personal trainer had paid off in the way of a sculpted legs and a tight ass. Now he wouldn't get to enjoy his investment. She stepped out of the closet with the dress in hand. His eyes roamed over the ensemble, and he stepped toward her. Her hand flung up. "Don't you even think about it." Did he honestly think that she'd just forget he'd stumbled into *their* bedroom with another woman?

"I loved you," she said. "I wanted to marry you." She foolishly thought that a Tiffany engagement ring was in their near future.

Daniel straightened his sleeves and smirked before meeting her eyes. "Did you honestly think I would marry you?"

His words were a heavy blow to her gut, knocking her back a step. "Yes," she said and hated the pathetic lilt in her tone.

"You were my intern."

Her hands landed on her hips, brushing against the expensive lace of her lingerie. "And now I'm your social media marketing specialist."

"Only because I couldn't let word get out that I was messing around with an intern. Do you know how bad that would've been for my company? For my reputation?"

"So what? You promoted me, so you could continue screwing me?"

He shrugged. "We were having fun, and I wasn't ready for it to end."

"Fun?" she exclaimed. "That's what's you're calling the last two years of our relationship?"

"Look, I know you're upset." He reached out to her, and she snatched her arm back. She didn't want his cheating hands anywhere near her. In fact, she'd given enough of herself, let him see more than his fair share. She yanked the designer dress over her head and let it slip into place.

"CEOs simply can't date interns. It's bad for business."

"But it wasn't just the job. You let me move in. You publicly called me your girlfriend and told me you loved me. I was your plus one at galas and charity events. I went to your father's funeral!"

"When it came out that we were together, I needed people to think it was a love match. Why else would I violate my own code of conduct? Making people believe you were the one created less scandal."

She shook her head. This wasn't happening. She'd been a pawn in his game the entire time, and she'd foolishly gone along with it? She helped him keep his squeaky-clean reputation while he used her, made her believe in true love and fairytales, all through lies and deception.

He used her. And worst of all, she'd let him.

She was too dumb to look beyond the penthouse apartment, designer clothes, unlimited pool of wealth and five-star accommodations. Oh god, did this make her a prostitute?

Her heart hammered her ribcage, her throat growing impossibly tight as she searched for words to throw in his face. She wanted to hurt him as badly as he hurt her, but words wouldn't hurt him. Rocks and a beating by a professional MMA fighter maybe, but words he'd wipe off. He was a cutthroat businessman who did what he had to do in order to get the job done. The only way to hurt him was to put a scuff in that clean reputation.

She didn't say anything as she pushed past him to grab her suitcase. He didn't try to stop her, not that she was surprised at this point. He'd gotten what he needed out of her already. She grabbed handfuls of clothes and shoes; she didn't care if he'd bought them for her. She looked at it as her consolation prize. Besides, half the items were worth more than what she had in her bank account right now.

She grabbed her Twist MM Louis Vuitton bag—her most prized possession; she'd bought it herself—and slung it on her arm. She closed her suitcase and zipped it shut.

"I'll send someone by to get the rest of my stuff," she said and slipped into her Louboutin heels.

"Where are you going? It's late."

"I guess I'm going home after all."

"At least take the car service."

Car service. Oh how she'd miss never having to wave a cab down again, especially in the freezing cold winters, but she'd manage. Then again, who knew where she'd be come winter...

She didn't want another thing from him. "I'll manage. And I think it's safe to say that I won't be at work on Monday. Consider this my resignation. Not that it matters, since the position was only created to cover up the fact that you were sleeping with your intern."

"Olivia," Daniel said, but she kept walking, dragging her suitcase behind her. He grabbed her elbow, and she yanked it from his grasp. He held his hands up and met her eyes. The soft blue had once set her world on fire, and now it was like ice reaching into her chest and freezing her heart. "Have coffee with me tomorrow."

Maybe he wanted to work things out. Maybe this was what he needed to realize that he did love her. That the last two years hadn't been a complete waste of her time.

"We can talk now," she said. Why put off till tomorrow what they could get out of the way right this second?

"I need time to discuss with my team how we should

go about releasing this to the public."

Her eyes snapped open, and her mouth practically hit the floor. "Excuse me?"

"We need to go about this diligently. Maybe even spin it to our benefit."

"Spin it?"

Her heart wasn't a damn business transaction of fodder for his reputation.

"Screw you!" Olivia stormed toward the elevator, ignoring Daniel's pleas. She tossed her suitcase inside and spun to him, pointing a perfectly manicured nail at his face. "I helped you keep your reputation under false pretenses, and maybe if I didn't love you, I would have seen the truth all along. But now I do. There is no way in hell I'll ever help you again. You want to keep your reputation intact? You should have thought about that before you had your hands up someone else's skirt."

She got on the elevator, and as soon as the doors closed, the feisty vengeful woman she'd transformed into seconds ago, collapsed into a pathetic, heartbroken fool.

***

Shane Sanchez McConnell got on the train at Jamaica station, heading to Morgan's Bay. He'd never been to the small town before, even though his father's side of the family owned the majority of the businesses, houses, and land. At least that's what his mother had told him before she died.

He didn't know his father, much less his family. It had always been just him and his mom, the dynamic duo, and that was all Shane had ever needed. He didn't need siblings;

Mom had enough on her plate with him, and he didn't need a dad because Mom had kept the memory of the man who helped create him alive. Shane had never met his father, but he felt as if he knew his father.

And now he would get to know his father's family—a family he never expected and wasn't exactly sure if he wanted. Family created ties and bonds, and he didn't want to burden anybody with his life. He'd already done that to Mom. Every day she was gone was a reminder of that.

The memory of her was swift and painful. He bit back the bitter regret of his life and walked down the aisle of the train. People filled the seats, but after a day of travel from car, to plane to train, he was exhausted and would settle for sitting on someone's lap at this point.

He continued down the aisle and sighed in relief when he spotted an open seat—other than the suitcase taking up the space. "Excuse me," he said to the woman who was staring out the window.

She turned, her black makeup smearing down her cheeks in sad lines. Her brown eyes were puffy and red. Her lip quivered, and she sucked in a ragged breath. He understood now why no one attempted to claim this seat as their own.

He offered her a smile, hoping it would bring some light into the gloomy night she was having. "Is this seat taken?"

"Sorry," she offered through a hiccup. "My bag is too big."

"That's no problem." He tossed his bag on the rack

above them and reached for hers. "I can toss it up with mine."

Her eyes filled with horror as if he suggested tossing her luggage out the back of the train and tying it to the wheel. "You don't understand; it's all I have left." She hugged the luggage to her chest, and he eyed her with curiosity.

"I can promise it's not going anywhere. I will be its personal security guard to make sure of it."

Her eyes drifted to the hot pink suitcase, her brown hair falling in her face. With a deep breath, she caught his eyes, and her lips curved into a smile. "If you promise."

He made an x motion over his heart, and she reluctantly let go of the suitcase. She nodded, and he gently placed the suitcase beside his before dropping into the seat. The LIRR didn't have the most comfortable seats in the world, but he was so tired that it didn't matter. A park bench would be a godsend after all his hours of travel.

His seatmate turned to the window, her shoulders shaking as a muffled sob escaped her. Shane hated to see people sad. Life was too short to let sorrow win.

"You okay?" he asked. Maybe the girl just needed someone to talk to, maybe occupy her mind for a little while.

She shifted in her seat, her brown eyes taking him in as a perfectly sculpted eyebrow arched. "You're not from the city, are you?"

His brows drew together. Even though he was born and raised in California, he didn't think he had a strong accent. "How'd you guess?"

"You're getting involved. People from here don't get in involved. We keep to ourselves."

Ignoring a stranger wasn't how he was raised. "That's a little rude."

"No, it's called respecting someone's privacy."

He glanced around the train before settling his gaze back on his seat mate. "It's kind of hard to be private when you're in the middle of a crowded train car, sobbing your eyes out."

"Which is why you keep to yourself…" She shook her head. "Never mind. You wouldn't understand."

"Because I'm not from around here?"

"Exactly. Now if you'll excuse me, I'm going to go back to my misery."

He let out a sigh and slumped down into his seat. "If you want to waste your time on frivolous emotions, be my guest."

Her gasp was audible through the train, causing a few heads to turn in their direction. "How do you even know what I'm upset about? What if I was crying because someone died? And you're over here being a jerk."

He held his hands up. "I'm not trying to be a jerk, but I know that's not why you're crying."

"How can you tell?"

"There's bitterness to your tone. You're crying more out of anger than sadness."

Her lips parted, but she didn't say anything. Probably because he got that nail right on the head. He'd been through grief; he knew the signs. Regardless if people grieved differently, the sadness was unmistakable.

"But I don't want to be rude," he said. "So, I'll let you get back to it." He popped earbuds in and didn't need to look at the woman to feel her penetrating gaze, glaring daggers in his direction. She flopped in the seat and rested into the headrest.

It'd been a long day, and it was just as well she wasn't the chatty type. He needed some sleep before he met his long-lost family. Especially since he'd be showing up five hours late, thanks to plane delays that were out of his control. One more inconvenience and he'd swear he was in a remake of *Planes, Trains and Automobiles*.

Still, he wouldn't let minor setbacks dampen his mood. After all, life was too short to waste it harping on bullshit. He closed his eyes and let the humming vibrations of the train lull him to sleep.

chapter 2

Ever since the out-of-towner sat beside her and inserted himself into her business, Olivia couldn't cry in peace. Was it too much to ask for a girl who had been cheated on and lost everything in the matter of minutes? So what if her tears were fueled by anger? Those tears deserved a release too, dammit, regardless of what Mr. Opinionated over there thought.

She glanced in his direction. He was good-looking; there was no denying that. Dark stubble lined his chiseled jawline, his nose made for a Grecian god, and his lips were perfectly plump on the bottom and bowed on top. He looked so peaceful with his eyes closed.

She wanted to drop her suitcase on his head. If she could no longer wallow in her pity, why should he be allowed to slumber into oblivion?

The anger he'd so kindly pointed out mixed with annoyance. She crossed her arms over her chest and let out a perturbed breath. One of his eyes popped open, and he angled his head in her direction.

"I'd ask if everything was okay, but I don't want to intrude on your misery."

"For your information, I was perfectly happy in my misery until you came along. Now I'm annoyed."

"You're welcome."

The audacity of some people still managed to stun her,

and she was a New Yorker! It took a special kind of person to possess that capability. "For what?" she demanded.

He lifted his strong, dominant chin. "No more tears."

She swiped at her eyes, and her fingers were dry. He was right. After he'd interjected himself into her business, she'd been too annoyed to cry. She didn't know if it was necessarily better, but at least she wasn't making a scene. Somehow, he managed to make her forget about Daniel and everything that transpired only a short time ago.

"Like I said, you're welcome."

"The next time you want to get someone to stop crying, maybe try a little compassion."

His other eye opened, and he sat up in his seat. "Hey, I tried to be nice, but you didn't exactly make it easy for me."

She sighed, and her shoulders slumped. "I'm sorry. I had a really rough night, and I know that's not your fault."

"I get it," he said, cutting her off from an inevitable word vomit with a side of too much information.

The train came to another stop, and she waited for him to grab his bag and head into the night. The door closed, and the train continued, and he was still there. Not many people stayed on to Morgan's Bay, at least not until after Memorial Day when the summer brought beach goers from the city.

"You didn't miss your stop, did you?" she asked.

"Nope. I'm riding this thing to the end."

She shifted in her seat. "You're going to Morgan's Bay?"

"Sure am."

She gave him a more thorough once over. She knew

every person who resided in Morgan's Bay—an easy feat when growing up in a small town that had the same families occupying the houses since the beginning of its founding.

"You're not from there," she stated.

"Nope."

"Then why are you going to Morgan's Bay?"

"Why do you care?"

Her small-town mentality kicked in, leaving the city girl behind her. "It's not the summer season yet, so the only reason people go to Morgan's Bay is because they live there or they know someone who lives there."

"If you say so."

"I do say so. So, who are you? Who do you know?" She could learn a lot about him based off those he was related to. Morgan's Bay was a small town, and just because Olivia had lived in the city for the last few years didn't mean she didn't have the four-one-one on pretty much every person who stepped foot in town.

"If I knew I was going to get the third degree I would've kept my earbuds in."

"Then lucky for me you took them out. So, go on. Out with it."

He sighed, running a hand over his face. "I'm meeting family I've never met before."

"Who are they? I can tell you everything you need to know about them." This just got interesting. She sat up in her chair and angled her body toward him, ready to give him the scoop.

He laughed. "I appreciate the offer, but I want to be

able to figure them out on my own. First impressions can tell a lot about a person, and I don't want to taint that with preconceived notions."

"If that were the case, then I don't even want to think what you might think about me. First impressions are not everything, and from my experience, nine times out of ten they're completely inaccurate."

His eyes darted to her, eyebrow lifting slightly. "Is that so?"

"Absolutely. The first time you meet someone, especially in a planned setting, they are on their best behavior."

He nodded and took his chin between thumb and forefinger. "How long does it take to finally know someone's true character?"

"I don't know. I lived with someone for two years and only found out who he truly was a few hours ago."

"Ouch."

"It's my own fault. I was so obsessed with the fairy tale that I couldn't see what was right in front of me the whole time."

"And what was that?"

"That he was a lying, manipulative, asshole who only cared about his career."

He held his hands up. "Sorry I asked."

"Don't be. I feel better now that it's off my chest." She didn't realize how much was building inside her until she opened the valve and let a little out. Maybe crying wasn't the best medicine. Maybe it was talking. Not that she was going to completely unload on this poor suspecting soul. She should just call her sister, but she'd been too embarrassed to earlier.

Cindy had the perfect life—so perfect she made a career out of it by posting pictures of her family on social media and starting a successful Mommy blog. Olivia didn't want to admit that she'd lost everything in the matter of minutes, but being only two years a part, Cindy had always been her rock.

"It's his loss."

Olivia turned to the handsome stranger and laughed. "I appreciate the sentiment, but I've been insufferable from the moment you got on this train. I bet in your head you think the guy dodged a bullet."

"You have spirit. That can be an admirable quality."

Her cheeks heated at the compliment. He had no reason to be nice to her now, but he was, and his kindness reminded her that just because Daniel was a dick didn't mean all men were. It was reassuring in a moment when she needed it most.

He checked his phone and leaned in the seat. "We have about another twenty minutes. Want to talk about it?"

Her head snapped around, practically flying off her neck. "You do not want to hear my sob story."

"My audiobook is done, and to be honest, your voice is much more pleasing than the narrator's."

She smiled. She'd ask him what book he was listening to, but she doubted she would know it. Daniel always got on her case for not reading more. He made her feel stupid, because she wasn't up-to-date on the newest entrepreneurial read. It wasn't her fault she preferred to spend her time reading fashion blogs and celebrity gossip rags.

"I'm Shane. Maybe knowing my name will make it easier to talk."

Any inhibitions she had slowly began to fade. "I'm Olivia."

"Now that we're best friends, let me have it."

"I have two best friends who would fight you for the title."

He smiled and it accentuated his handsome features. "We don't want that."

"No, they fight dirty." He laughed and the sound was the final wave of calm she needed. "You sure you want to hear about this disaster?"

"Lay it on me."

With a deep breath, she started. Each declaration, every word brought her farther from the pain and heartache. She passed through a level of pissed off she didn't realize was clinging inside of her then ended on a strange mixture of regret and relief. Regret for allowing Daniel to string her along for so long, and relief for finally getting everything that happened tonight out of her mind. She'd been wallowing in her own pool of pity. She wasn't ready to get out of the pool completely. Maybe after a few chocolate bars and cocktails, she'd feel differently.

She glanced at Shane who was listening to her intently. She threw her hands up and let them fall into her lap. "And that's how I lost everything in the matter of minutes, and now I'm heading home with my tail tucked between my legs, moving in with my parents while I try to figure out what's next."

"Not going to lie, that sucks."

"Pretty much."

"But it also looks like a blessing in disguise."

That blessing must've been in full costume. "How is any of this a blessing?"

"You can start from scratch."

"Again, how is that a blessing?"

"You have a chance to do it differently. Maybe do it right this time." The tone of his voice made her wonder if that was exactly what he was doing himself. She was about to ask when the train came to a stop.

"Look at that. Finished just in time."

But now that she was talking to him, she didn't want to stop. She wanted to know who his family was. She wouldn't even spill the beans about what she knew of them; she was just curious who he was getting off the train to go meet. And how he was related to them? There were so many possibilities. Her brain started working, trying to piece it together.

He stood and grabbed her luggage, taking it down for her.

"Thank you. I could have gotten it."

"I'm the reason it was up there. Taking it down is the least I could do."

Now that her claws weren't out, she could see the nice guy he really was. "Do you have a ride to wherever you're going?" she asked.

"I was going to call a cab."

She bit her lip to hold back a laugh. He really wasn't from around here. "We don't have cabs in Morgan's Bay, but we do have our own car ride service. I already called him. We can share if you want. Or you can wait until he drops me off then comes back to get you." Milo wouldn't mind. He created his business because he liked meeting people and talking.

"If you don't mind."

She met his eyes, looking at them for the first time, and startled by the intensity in his brown gaze. "Not at all."

"Lead the way." He stepped out of the seat and let her into the aisle. She went to grab her bag, but he waved her off. "I got it."

She didn't know if she was just relieved that he wasn't an asshole, or if he was genuinely a nice guy. Either way, she was happy to have her faith restored in men, even if it was only for tonight.

His arm muscle flexed beneath his t-shirt as he took the weight of the bag in his hold before placing it on the ground. He pulled on the handle and stood there when she realized she was blocking the way. She spun around and headed toward the exit.

The fresh clean salt air rushed over her. It didn't give her that excited jolt like stepping out into the industrial fueled air of the city, but it did wrap around her in a familiar embrace that relaxed her shoulders and had her walking a little slower.

Shane followed her down the platform. Without the hustle and bustle of the city, the sound of the luggage rolling along the cement rumbled through the dark night.

Olivia glanced toward the parking lot and immediately spotted Milo's red Nissan Altima parked at the curb. Milo was the only car service in Morgan's Bay and happened to be one of Olivia's good friends. He leaned against the hood of his car under a streetlight, arms crossed over his chest, the logo of his family's business, Amato Construction, poking out above his bicep. His chestnut hair was a stylish, disheveled mess as usual, and his smile reminded her why home was the best place for her right now.

"Look what the train dragged home," Milo said and pushed off the car. Olivia laughed and hurried to him. He opened his arms wide, and she went willingly. He smelled like the ocean, like home, and she held onto him for a moment, relishing in the comfort of a friendly hug. It was exactly what she needed to end her less than stellar night.

Milo pulled back and studied her face. "Normally I'd say you look good, but unless this black cheek streak is a new trend I haven't heard about, you look like hell, Liv."

Olivia choked on a laugh and punched him in the shoulder. "Shut up, Milo. I had a bad night."

"Is that all? Looks more like a bad month."

"Don't make me deck you." She balled up her fist and held it in front of him in a menacing but playful way. "You know I will."

"Oh, I know." He rubbed at his cheek. "Can still feel the pain from that day in eighth grade."

"You deserved it." The dumbass pretended he was drowning and nearly gave not only her but Harper and Isla heart attacks. He found it hilarious, and Olivia needed to show him how funny they thought his little prank was.

"Does Harper know you're home?" Harper was one of Olivia's best friends, and she liked to joke with Milo that he could only borrow Harper, but the truth was no matter how close Olivia and Harper were and they were practically sisters, Harper and Milo shared a special bond. It was why they also shared a house, though, Harper swore she never slept with Milo. "I thought she said you decided to stay in the city this weekend."

"Change of plans," Olivia said.

Shane cleared his throat, and Olivia was grateful for the interruption. Even though she'd unloaded on Shane, she didn't want to spill her guts to Milo yet. She wanted to hold onto the last bit of dignity she had for a little while longer.

Milo nodded toward Shane. "Can I help you?"

"Oh!" Olivia exclaimed. "This is Shane. He's in town for a visit and needs a lift, too. I said he could share the car with me."

"You only put down one passenger. Not two."

Olivia rolled her eyes. "Consider it a friend helping out a friend."

"Is he a friend I don't know about?"

"I'm talking about you helping me… never mind. You're giving him a ride."

"I don't want to impose," Shane said. "I'm sure I can find a way."

Olivia held her hand up and flashed Milo the evil eye. "Nonsense. Milo is just being difficult." The least she could do was get the guy a ride after that disastrous train ride.

Milo ignored Olivia and swung his gaze to Shane. "Who are you visiting?"

Olivia shoved Milo in the chest, pushing him toward the back of the car. "Don't be so nosy."

"But—"

Olivia cut Milo another look, this time with more finality behind it, and he sighed before walking toward the trunk. The occasional limp he had after being hit by a drunk driver the summer of senior year, destroying his baseball career, was barely noticeable except to those who knew him. "Fine, let's go. But I'll have to know where he's going if he ever wants to get there."

Olivia gave Shane a smile, and he thanked her with a nod. Shane had made it perfectly clear on the train that he didn't want to know anything about his family before he met them. She wasn't about to give that opening to Milo who would undoubtedly share every opinion he ever had.

Milo popped the trunk, and Shane deposited the bags. Olivia took the backseat, since she was used to being chauffeured around, but also she figured Shane as the newbie to the area, could take the front seat. Plus, after putting up with her on the train, it was the least she could do.

Shane stood outside the car for a moment, and Milo leaned over from the driver seat and pushed open the passenger door. "You can sit up here, my man."

Shane climbed into the car, and Olivia slid over to his side. She settled behind him and leaned toward the gap between seat and door. "I'll be your tour guide," she said. She knew every nook and cranny in this town. "I know all the best places to get coffee, the best place to get a bacon, egg and cheese, and the best place to grab a cocktail."

"That's because there's only one of each," Milo said.

She caught Milo's dark brown eyes in the rearview mirror. "Nobody asked you."

"It's kind of hard to take you serious when you look like Hal when he's dressed up for a gig." Hal was a town celebrity—an Alice Cooper impersonator who performed at any local business that would let him.

Olivia shifted so she could see herself in the rearview mirror and gasped at the fact she allowed herself to look like that in public. Even more surprised Shane didn't hightail it away from her the minute he saw her face.

"You thought I was lying?" Milo joked.

Olivia tapped Shane on the shoulder. "Why didn't you say anything to me?"

He turned around in his seat to face her, but because she was already leaning close, they were a few breaths away from each other. His eyes met hers, and while she thought they were brown, up close and really looking at him, she could see they were also green.

He shrugged. "You were already upset. I didn't want to make it worse."

It was simple, nothing really, but the fact that a stranger cared enough not to upset her more squeezed at her heart.

She held his gaze, wondering about the mysterious Shane and what he was doing in her hometown.

First time visiting our lovely town?" Milo's voice cut through the moment, and Olivia dropped her gaze, leaning back in her seat.

Shane nodded. "First time on the east coast actually."

Milo put his blinker on and turned out of the parking lot. "Let me guess… a Cali guy?"

Shane's head tilted toward his solid navy-blue tee and tan shorts as if he was trying to figure out how Milo guessed correctly. Olivia was curious herself. She didn't see any insignia on Shane's clothes, then again, she spent an entire train ride with him and didn't notice his brown eyes also had a pretty shade of green.

"Good guess," Shane said, and Olivia eyed the back of Milo's head.

Milo shot Shane an amused look. "The LAX tag on your luggage kind of gave it away."

Shane sighed. "For a second there I thought maybe you were psychic."

"Psycho maybe," Olivia chimed in. "Oh!" She tapped on the window as they made a turn. "This is Main Street. Most of the local businesses can be found here. At the four corners you can find the McConnell Pharmacy and the McConnell Pub. Next to the pharmacy is the McConnell Market and next to the pub is—"

"I'm guessing another McConnell place," Shane said.

"You sure you haven't been here?" she asked, her cheeks warming as he looked over his shoulder and caught her eye between the seat and the door.

"Maybe he's psychic," Milo said.

"Keep your eyes on the road." She turned to the window then glanced at Shane. "It's McConnell Hardware. There are not many places left that the McConnell's don't own in this town. There's this silly rule in the town that's been around since the beginning that states you can only buy a house here if you're a descendant of an original town founder. Patrick McConnell has taken advantage of that rule and scoops up property faster than it can go on the market then rents it out. He's been trying to build a big fancy hotel down by the beach for years, but luckily the mayor won't let him."

"Isn't the mayor—"

"His son," Olivia finished for him. "Yup. Looks like you've done your research."

"A little."

"I bet holidays are a blast in that big house on the bay," Milo said as he brought the car to a stop at a stop sign.

"With as much money as they have, I'm sure they're all just fine," Olivia said. Based on her current predicament, she was living proof that money didn't buy happiness, but for a while it had brought her security and a freedom that she would no longer have. No, money didn't buy her happiness, but at least she could drown herself in the racks at Saks. Now all she had was her old bedroom in her parents' house while she tried to figure out how to pick up the pieces.

Milo hitched a thumb in Olivia's direction. "Liv over here is a little obsessed with the McConnell's."

"Am not."

"She's basically trying to become one. Between the fancy boyfriend, living in a penthouse in Manhattan, visiting us peasants on her way home from a gala in the Hamptons… Bayview, the McConnell family estate, is her dream home. She used to talk for hours about how one day she'd live in a house just like that." Olivia flicked Milo's ear, and his head retracted like a turtle going into his shell. "Ouch. What was that for?"

"You talk too much." She sunk in her seat. "The house is beautiful is all," Olivia said. "Anybody would want to live there."

She didn't want Shane to think she was shallow. She wasn't. Not at all. There was nothing wrong with enjoying the finer things and living a life she'd always dreamed of. Not that it mattered anymore. That life was in the rearview mirror. She couldn't afford rent on a studio apartment let alone a waterfront estate.

She wasn't ready to think about it, so when Milo slowed down in front of Bay's Bagels Olivia went back into tour guide mode.

"Bay's Bagels have the best bacon, egg and cheese on the island. I dream about them when I'm not home. They're that good. McConnell's Pub has karaoke on Thursday nights, but Mrs. Littleton usually dominates the stage with ballad after ballad, so most people avoid it, unless they want to grab their half off apps and special drink menu. Sometimes it's almost worth it. Sometimes."

Milo continued at a snail pace, letting Olivia point out

all the places to Shane. "Here before Morcant Circle is Aunt Greta's diner, home of the best pancakes you'll ever eat, and I can't forget their vanilla milkshakes. They are the best I've ever had, and I have had a lot of milkshakes in my life."

"I'll have to stop by. Vanilla milkshakes are my favorite."

"Mine too." Warmth spread through Olivia's cheeks when Shane looked at her. "Maybe we can grab one together sometime."

What the hell was she doing? She was newly single—definitely not looking for a date.

"As friends of course," she added, hoping it didn't sound like she was trying to cover up when he didn't immediately respond.

"Maybe after I settle in," he said, and Olivia sighed a breath of relief.

"Who are you fooling?" Milo asked. "The last time I saw you drink a milkshake was in tenth grade before everything became empty calories that'll make your ass fat."

Olivia cut Milo a look, not that it would deter him. "For your information, for the last six months I have worked with one of the best personal trainers—who also works with some very famous clientele—to get my ass in check, and he told me I'm allowed cheat days."

And after the disastrous night she just had, she had many cheat meals in her future.

Milo followed the traffic circle and took the last exit for Harbor Hill Lane. The closer she got to her childhood home, the heavier her heart was. She'd made a promise to herself a long time ago that she would get out of this town. Going back at twenty-five was not part of her plan, and she couldn't help but feel like a complete and total failure.

Unfortunately, with little to no savings, thanks to one too many shopping sprees, this was her only option. She'd bounce back. There was no way she was staying in this town longer than she had to.

Milo pulled up to the house—an 1840's farmhouse with brown, weathered shingles and a light blue door. A white picket fence surrounded the property.

"Thank you for riding with me on this lovely evening. My name is Milo Amato, and it has been my pleasure to be your driver."

Olivia rolled her eyes. "Needs work before tourist season starts."

"Damn, thought I had it."

The front door opened, and embarrassment flared red hot in Olivia's cheeks. The outside light turned on, highlighting Dad as he stepped out in a white undershirt tucked into a pair of wide opened jeans and the band of his tighty-whities. On his feet were a pair of green monster slippers that her niece had picked out for his Christmas gift. Olivia never thought he'd actually wear them, but there he was, standing in the doorway, hand on his head, squinting toward the car. His other arm he held Olivia's fur brother, John Andre, who her father named after the British Spy. According to Dad, the Yorkie had charmed his way into their lives.

"Olivia is that you?" Dad called out, his voice muffling

against the closed window but still loud and very clear. As a history teacher, he had a way of making his voice project across any space.

Fresh air seeped into the car, and Olivia turned to see Milo rolling the window down. "Hi, Mr. Green," Milo called out. "Love your slippers."

The heat in Olivia's cheeks exploded, fiery trails shooting down her neck and into her chest.

"Milo Amato, is that you?"

"Sure is!"

"Thank you for giving my daughter a ride."

"Anytime, Mr. Green."

Okay that was enough. Olivia jumped out of the car, using her body to block Shane's view of Dad's fashion faux paus. "Hi, Dad. You can go back in. I'll be right behind you."

"Do you need money to pay Milo?"

"No, Dad. I already took care of it."

"Did you tip him?"

Olivia pinched the bridge of her nose, attempting to ward off a headache. "Dad, I got it!"

"You sure?"

"Yes." Olivia tried her hardest not to snap. She loved her father, but sometimes he tested her patience. "I'll be right in," she called over her shoulder. "Please go inside," she mumbled under her breath. Olivia turned around, hoping to all that was holy that Dad wasn't waiting for her in the doorway.

She sighed in relief when she spotted his retreating

frame.

Milo reached down and popped the trunk. "You got your bag, right?"

"I'll get it," Shane offered, and Olivia bit back a smile as Shane got out of the car. Luckily Dad had gone back in the house with John Andre.

"Look at that, Milo." Olivia bent down to the window. "A real gentleman."

"You know me," Milo said. "I have nothing to prove to you."

"Tell Harper I'll call her in the morning."

"When she gets home from her date."

"Another date? Who now?"

"Another online guy. This one says he's an entrepreneur. She got mad at me when I told her it was a fancy way of saying unemployed."

"I don't know why she's so determined to meet someone," Olivia said.

"She doesn't want to wind up like her mom."

Olivia never thought about it, but Milo was probably right. Harper's mom was a bit of a mess, jumping from one guy to the next, never happy, always wanting more, and drinking herself to sleep when she couldn't find it… which was often. "That'll never happen."

"You know that, and I know that." Milo waved a finger between them. "But you know her."

"There's no talking to her."

"Exactly why I'm staying out of it."

Milo might not have questioned Harper's quest for

love, but he definitely wasn't out of it. He was there for her after every date gone wrong to lift her spirits.

"I can bring it up to the door for you if you'd like," Shane said, and Olivia spun toward him.

"I can manage."

"You sure?" He glanced down at her shoes.

She kicked up her foot, examining the stiletto before placing it back on the ground. "I walked through Penn Station in heels. I've got this."

"Well, it was nice meeting you."

Olivia's cheeks warmed. If someone would have told her a couple hours ago that there'd be a bright spot in her night, she wouldn't have believed them. But here he was, standing right in front of her, being polite even after their horrible initial interaction. "Sorry I was such a hot mess."

"Put it this way, I've already seen you at your worst. It can only go up from there."

"Does that mean you plan on seeing me again?" she asked, surprised at the flirtatious tone in her voice.

He smiled, his gaze bashfully dropping to the ground before meeting hers straight on. "From what you said, it's a small town. I'm sure I'll see you around." He winked at her, and her heart sputtered in place.

Shane got back in the car, and she leaned down to the window. "Be nice, Milo."

"Always am." He turned to Shane. "So where are we off to?"

"Bayview Estate, my grandparent's house." Shane said, and Olivia lost her balance. Her eyes locked on his, and confusion swirled into annoyance. She'd gone on and on about the McConnell's, and he didn't think to chime in once to say he himself was one.

Shane shrugged, and before she could gather her thoughts, Milo pulled away, his laughter floating out the window in his wake.

chapter 3

Earlier Olivia had moved quickly for someone in heels as if the added height was a part of her, but now Shane watched her as Milo pulled away. The cupid bow-shape of her mouth hung open like she was halted in thought. Maybe he should have told her who he was, but he enjoyed listening to her and was intrigued by her take on the family he would be meeting for the first time.

The interior of the car still held her scent—a combination that was both fruity and floral that had him inhaling to savor the aroma a little longer. It was almost calming, just as she'd been. He'd been a bucket of nerves all day, hiding behind the story in his ears, until he sat next to Olivia on the train.

As standoffish as she was in the beginning, it was almost a breath of fresh air to see someone wear their emotions so openly. It's not something he did. He learned at a very young age to keep his emotions to himself; he didn't want Mom to worry any more than she had to.

Being diagnosed with leukemia at ten was terrifying, but he'd always been the man of the house, and he didn't let the fear of the disease change that. Not even when he heard Mom crying late at night when she had thought he was asleep.

Speaking with Olivia, he was able to lose himself in her

problems and forget about his own for a moment. That sliver of time with her was calming in a way he never would have predicted, based on their first interaction.

"How long will you be in town?" Milo asked, and Shane glanced from the window, meeting his eyes.

"Not sure. I guess it depends on if I like my family or not."

"I've lived in Morgan's Bay my entire life, and I'd be lying if I told you the McConnell's didn't have a reputation around here."

"How so?" The closer Shane got to the house, the more his curiosity piqued.

"Considering they own much of the town they aren't exactly neighborly. Okay… that's not entirely true. Some members of the family are very active here in the community. Not sure where you fall on the family tree, but the mayor is a good guy. He started out running the local pub until he ran for office and passed the torch to his son. And Connor is cool is hell. We go way back. Those two I'd share a drink with."

"What about my grandfather?"

Milo went silent for a second, his head tilted, and he sucked in a breath through his teeth. "The not exactly neighborly comment could probably lay solely on his shoulders. The McConnell's have owned much of the area since the founding of the town, but your grandfather expanded into real estate, scooping up more properties, constantly trying to bring luxury apartments to the beach front. Luckily, the mayor sides with the townspeople and has been successful at shutting him down."

"Isn't the mayor his son?"

Milo smirked. "Seems to be a long, complicated history."

"Great." What was Shane stepping into?

"But," Milo said, "it's all speculation. No one knows what actually happens behind the doors of Bayview. It's easy to create drama looking in from the outside."

"You said you and Connor go way back. You've never been inside the house?"

Milo laughed. "The only people allowed in that house are the type who consider paying four hundred dollars for a steak reasonably priced. That would be a massive chunk of my weekly salary, and I have bills to pay. I've been to Connor's place plenty of times, though. He used to have the best birthday parties back in elementary school."

The only birthday parties Shane remembered were in the children's hospital. He'd spent so much time there everything before seemed like a distant dream.

"You really have known him for a long time then." It amazed Shane this total stranger who had no relation to his cousin knew Connor better than Shane did.

Milo nodded. "Most people in this town have known each other for a long time. The curse of small-town life. Most people want to escape, and others never want to leave."

"Where do you fall on that line?"

"It doesn't matter. I'll be here for the rest of my life just like my dad and just like my grandfather." There was defeat in his tone, as if he'd tried and failed, or maybe he'd given up. Either way, Shane felt for the guy. He knew what it was like to feel stuck. It was why he easily accepted the invitation to visit Morgan's Bay. After losing a great deal of his childhood and the one constant in his life, he was ready to be free. He decided saying yes was the only way to break the shackles holding him in the misery of his past.

Milo brought the car to a stop in front of a wrought iron fence that extended the length of a massive waterfront property. It was hard to see the house from the end of the long driveway, but Shane imagined it was like nothing he'd ever have the privilege to step into before.

"Here it is… Bayview Estate. It has the best views of the bay from every angle of the house. At least that's what I've heard."

"Thanks. How much do I owe you?" Shane reached into his back pocket for his wallet.

"The ride was charged to Olivia's account."

Shane went to argue, and Milo held his hand up.

"Don't worry about it. Her boyfriend is loaded. He pays her way for the most part."

"According to her, they broke up."

Milo's eyes widened. "That explains why she's home. Huh. You would think Harper would've mentioned it to me."

"It sounds very recent. Like last few hours recent."

"Then man am I happy you met her, or I would have had to listen to the whole story."

Shane laughed.

"Don't get me wrong," Milo said. "I love that girl. She's the best. But I don't do well when girls cry. I always say the wrong thing then they hate me."

From what Shane could tell, Milo seemed like a pretty nice guy. Friendly, charismatic… all the qualities that made up a good person. He couldn't imagine anyone hating the guy.

"Thanks for giving me a lift. I know I wasn't originally on your ticket."

"I was just busting on Liv. It was no problem."

Milo was the type of guy Shane could be friends with, but he didn't know how long he was staying, and friendship was the exact type of entanglement he avoided. Shane had had plenty of friends; unfortunately spending the majority of his youth in and out of children's hospital, many of his friends had succumbed to their illness.

He always assumed he'd be next, especially after the phone would ring, and Mom would console the grieving parent on the other end. But for whatever reason, he'd survived. Life was fragile, though, and he knew at any minute the cancer that had lived inside of him could rear its ugly head and finally take him out. The doctors had said he beat it. It'd been more than five years, but he could never let go of what a doctor had said to Mom when she had been hopeful.

You're never fully cancer free. It was bullshit. Shane had met plenty of people who went into remission and had yet to have another bout, but those words still haunted him.

He tried not to think about it. Making friends,

attachments put the thoughts to the forefront of his mind. Which was why he avoided making friends in the first place. No friends meant neither side had to deal with the emotional pitfalls of loss.

"Thanks again," Shane said. He got out of the car and went to the trunk to grab his bag. He hiked it on his shoulder, shut the trunk, and gave the car a good tap.

Milo pulled away with a wave, and Shane stood at the wrought iron gate in front of him. When he had told the woman that was his grandmother—still a hard concept for him to grasp—that he'd be late, she'd given him the gate code. He punched that into the keypad, and the large gate opened.

He made his way up the driveway. It was dark, and he couldn't see the property around him, but he could smell the salt in the air, hear the water in the distance, and sense that the land around him was massive.

To think all the times Mom had struggled to pay the bills, yet he had family who lived in a place like this. The thing Shane couldn't figure out was that Mom knew they existed, so why didn't she ask them for help?

He knew the answer before he even finished the thought. Mom had been a proud person, asking for money from anyone made her feel inferior. She didn't see it as someone helping her out; she saw it as her own inadequacy. She'd been stubborn that way. As a child Shane didn't understand it, but as an adult, he respected it.

Shane continued up the driveway, moving past the trees that blocked the estate. Bayview Estate wasn't as opulent as he expected. It was large, yet cozy. Weathered brown shingles, similar to those on Olivia's house, covered the house, but instead of the rustic look of Olivia's house, these shingles made the estate look like old money. White trim accented the windows on the house and the large turret that sat in the middle of the structure.

The fact that he wasn't met with an excessive display of wealth was a bit of a relief. In his head, he was starting to believe his family were a bunch of rich assholes, which would explain why his dad had taken off all those years ago, but now he hoped that they were just everyday people who happened to have a ton of money.

He confidently approached the front door, and before he could chicken out, he knocked. He only waited a moment before the door flung open.

A woman who looked like Goldie Hawn, both in face and stature, stood in the doorway. Her mouth dropped into an O, and she gasped.

He shifted uncomfortably from one foot to the other as she continued to stare. "Hi, I'm Shane."

Tears filled her blue eyes, and her hands landed on her tightly pulled skin. "Look at you. Just like your father. My baby boy." Her overly plump lip quivered, and she pulled him into an embrace. He didn't resist, finding her hold rather comforting.

Her scent was strong but pleasant—definitely expensive. She cried against his shoulder, and he patted her back. "It's okay, Grandma. No need to cry."

She sniffled and pulled back; the tears halted in her

eyes. "I am nobody's grandma."

"I…" Shane stuttered.

"Call me Mimi."

"Six grandkids, and she still can't accept that she's old." A middle-aged man walked into the room; his light brown hair streaked with gray was brushed to the side and off his face. Shane imagined his own eyes would look like this man's if they had been all green and not a mix of green and brown.

"Do I look like a grandmother?" She planted her hand on her popped hip and tilted her head.

"Not any I've met," Shane said.

Mimi let out a loud laugh. "A charmer, just like your father." Shane hadn't been trying to charm her; he was just being honest.

The man walked into the room and draped his arm over Mimi's shoulders, kissing her cheek. Mimi smiled. "This is your world, and you're nice enough to let us live in it." The man's arms dropped from Mimi, and he held a hand to Shane. "I'm your Uncle Grady."

Uncle Grady had a strong grip, which told Shane a lot about his character. He was a professional, obviously. He *was* the town mayor. Shane recognized him from a picture he found on a Google search.

"How are you feeling? You look good. Strong, healthy."

"I'm feeling great," Shane said. They were odd first words for an uncle meeting his nephew. Then again, Shane didn't know much about this family.

Uncle Grady patted his shoulder. "That's good. That's really good. Come on, I'll give you a ride over to the house, and you can get settled. We can get to know each other a little better after you get some rest."

"What house?" Shane asked.

"I thought you'd be more comfortable in your own space," Mimi said. "We have a ton of rentals around town, and one is currently empty, so we thought you could stay there."

"Oh, I couldn't—"

Mimi cut him off with a wave. "Don't be ridiculous."

"That's very generous."

"You're family. My grandson." Mimi cupped his cheek, her hand the only thing giving away her true age.

Shane appreciated the gesture, but he didn't come here to live off his rich family. His pride wouldn't let him. "I'd like to at least try and get a job while I'm in town."

Mimi patted his cheek. Her look of admiration made him uneasy, like he was some gift from God. He didn't want to disappoint her, but there wasn't anything special about him. He was an average guy who was a little more damaged than most.

"I think we can help him with that, don't you?" Mimi said to Uncle Grady.

"Definitely. You don't want to work with me at Town Hall, but I'll tell you what. Your cousin, Connor would love to meet you, and he happens to be short a bartender right now. Last guy up and left to follow a girl across the country."

"That would be awesome. Thanks." Shane knew nothing about his cousin, but from what Milo had said,

Connor seemed like a good guy. Not that he knew Milo from a hole in the wall, but the guy had no reason to lie.

"Stop at McConnell's Pub tomorrow around noon, and I'll tell him you're coming."

Mimi clapped. "Now that's arranged, go get settled, and we'll meet tomorrow first thing for coffee and breakfast before you head over to the pub. Then you can tell me about the last twenty-five years."

"Not much to tell, but I'd love to talk about my dad. Know what he was like, why he left."

She hugged him and pulled back, taking his face in her hands again. "I'm so happy you're here."

"Me too, but—" He stopped himself. He had a million questions about his dad and this new family, but it had been a long day of travel and it was late. The answers weren't going anywhere. He would get some sleep, and come back tomorrow, awake and prepared to find out about the father who died before he was born.

Chapter 4

Olivia finished putting her makeup on, trying to hide the puffiness from a night and early morning of crying. It didn't do much, but it was better than nothing. Mom would know she'd been crying the moment Olivia left her room, and no amount of makeup in the world could change that.

Her phone rang, and she glanced down to see her sister's name flash on the screen. She hadn't been ready to talk, but she also couldn't avoid Cindy forever. She accepted the call and put the phone to her ear.

"Hey, Cind."

"Hey. How are you holding up?"

Olivia paused. She hadn't even had a chance to tell her sister about what had happened. She'd been avoiding it like a bad habit. "You talked to Mom, didn't you?"

"I called her this morning, and she might have mentioned something."

"Is anything sacred in this family?" God forbid Mom held onto a bit of information for longer than twenty-four hours. Olivia should have known she might have combusted if she tried.

"Twenty-five years old and you still question this?"

"It still amazes me that Mom can spread gossip so quickly."

"As Mom says, words between family isn't gossip, just the transferring of information."

"We both know that's her way to justify her inability to keep a secret."

"How are you settling in?" Cindy asked, moving right to the next subject at hand. Cindy was a to-the-point type of person.

"It's like a time warp. Everything is exactly how I left it, and I feel sixteen again." Olivia had been back a million times over the years, but now that she was here to stay, the blast from the past was unsettling. Especially the dream board that held magazine clippings glued to it of Madison Ave, New York City penthouse apartments, designer bags, and Blair Waldorf from Gossip Girl—Olivia's favorite television show in high school.

Her entire life was focused on moving forward, reaching for the top, and now she was back at the bottom. This wasn't how it was supposed to be.

"At least they didn't turn your room into the dog's room," Cindy spat.

Shortly after Cindy moved out to live with her fiancé, now husband, Mom and Dad moved John Andre into her room. Now the room was filled with a toybox full of dog toys, two beds, and a painting of John Andre hung on the far wall.

"Still not over that, huh?"

"Do you know Mom made him filet mignon for dinner the other night. Filet mignon! We used to get tossed ten bucks and told to call for pizza."

"We weren't fluffy and adorable."

"I don't know what you're talking about. I was adorable

and still am." And she had over a million followers who agreed, but Olivia was her sister, and it was her job to knock her down a few notches every chance she got.

"You're all right."

"Gee thanks."

"Anytime. Besides, it's not about you right now. Your life is perfect. Can we focus on the disaster that is my life?"

Olivia swore eye rolls made noise, and Cindy just made a very dramatic roll. "If we must."

"Why do I like you again?" Olivia asked.

"Because you're my sister, and you have no choice."

"Good point."

"But seriously… How are you holding up?"

"I cried for twenty minutes in the shower this morning before Dad knocked on the door to remind me I was using all the hot water."

"Oil's expensive," Cindy snapped.

Olivia's brow furrowed at the hostility in Cindy's tone. She expected her sister to laugh with her or at least commiserate with her over the intrusion. "Geez, didn't know you were paying their oil bill."

"I'm just saying, as a homeowner, I get it."

"And because I don't own a home, I don't?" This was exactly why Olivia came home instead of crashing at Cindy's. Cindy, while always there for her, had a way of making Olivia feel as if she was too immature in life to understand responsibilities, all because she wasn't married with a house and kid. "Besides they don't have oil burners in skyrises."

Cindy sighed into the phone. "That's not what I meant,

and you know it.”

Olivia inhaled slowly. She was projecting. “You’re right. I’m sorry. I’m a little on edge.”

“You just went through a breakup. Give yourself a little time.”

“It’s not just that, Cin. I’m twenty-five, no career, no place of my own, no savings. I have nothing, and I have no idea how I let myself get here.”

“It’s part of life. Not everything can be up. Sometimes we have to be dropped down a few pegs to realize what we have. Harsh lessons are the best ones. At least you’re twenty-five and single. You only have to worry about you right now. And don’t take that as an insult, because it’s not. Take a few weeks, a month, the entire summer if you have to. There’s no rush. You’ll figure it out when the time is right.”

“I don’t know if I’ll last the entire summer with Mom and Dad.”

“Look at it as a test of your endurance.” Cindy laughed. At least she could find the humor in her parental hell; Olivia didn’t share her sentiment.

“I’m glad you can laugh about this.”

“You will. In due time. I’ll be out that way on Wednesday. We can grab coffee, talk.”

“I’d like that.”

“See you then.”

“Kiss my niece for me.”

“I will.” Olivia hung up and took a moment before heading downstairs and facing her parents.

John Andre met her at the stairs, butt wiggling back

and forth, nose sniffing her feet before he flopped on his back, legs up in prime petting position.

"Hey, good boy!" Olivia said, giving John Andre exactly what he wanted. She rubbed his belly and scratched behind his ears, and when she straightened to continue, he quickly stood and dropped down on her feet. She grabbed the wall before she would be forced to join him on the floor. "I'm sorry. Were we not done here?" Olivia gave him a few more rubs and scratches and finally an acceptable amount of attention for the spoiled Yorkie. He rolled over and waited for Olivia to lead.

With a laugh she made her way into the kitchen.

Dad was at the table, newspaper in hand. Olivia had been trying to get him to go digital forever, but he refused to give up the feel of paper in his hands in the morning. His green monster slippers poked out from beneath the table, and Olivia shook her head at the monstrosities.

"Morning," Olivia said as she followed the scent of coffee to the pot. John Andre was on her heels, so she grabbed the two bags of treats and placed them on the floor. "Which one do you want?" John Andre sniffed both bags then pawed the bag with the peanut butter bones. "Good choice." Olivia fished out a bone and tossed it into the living room. John Andre took off, grabbed the bone, and instantly went to find a place to hide it.

"Coffee is brewing, and your mother went to get bagels," Dad said, from behind the paper.

Olivia poured herself a cup and went to grab the almond milk out of the fridge, only to remember her parents only drank whole milk. She snatched the gallon container. She still had a little money in her checking account and could afford a run to McConnell's Market to stock up on the necessities.

She dropped a scoop of sugar into her mug, making a mental note to pick up a bag of raw sugar, then leaned against the counter. The first sip was like heaven, and she took a moment to savor it before nodding to Dad's feet.

"I bought you shearling lined, suede slippers last year, and you refuse to wear them."

"For all the money you spent on those things, they weren't comfortable. You could have put that money into savings, and you might not be in this predicament."

Annoyance flared beneath the surface, and Olivia took a deep breath. "Two hundred dollars wouldn't have made a difference."

He folded the paper and placed it down on the table. "Maybe not. But think of all the other unnecessary purchases you've made over the years. They add up. What about your purse? Your sister told me it's a few thousand dollars." His eyes widened, and he laughed. "A few thousand dollars," his words came out in a high-pitched squeak. "For a bag!"

That bag was her most prized possession. Daniel's money didn't buy it. It was the first big purchase she'd ever made, and she'd been so proud when she was able to go up to the register and hand over her debit card. So what if it left her with only a hundred bucks in her checking account? She finally got to be one of the women walking down Fifth Avenue who stopped in the Louis Vuitton store and made a purchase on a random Wednesday because she could. With the last hundred bucks, she took herself and the bag out for champagne rose macaroons and a latte.

Maybe Dad had a point. That money would have really helped her out, but she wouldn't regret that purchase or the macaroons after. That day was empowering, and it gave her a little extra bounce in her step. The experience, the feeling made it worth the money, despite the uncertainty she faced now.

"Can we not talk about this right now? My life is in shambles, and I don't need to be reminded about all the things I've done to get me here."

Dad ran a hand over his thick mustache that he'd been sporting all of Olivia's life. "Then let's talk about what you're going to do to get you back on track."

Olivia sighed. She loved her father, but he didn't understand the need to take a moment. When something didn't work out, he was quick to come up with a new plan. Olivia didn't have a plan yet, and the last thing she wanted was to discuss it. She needed to figure out her next steps on her own and in her own time. "Can't I have a day to not think?"

Dad reached across the table and took her hand, giving it a squeeze. "I worry about you."

"I know," Olivia said.

Concern pinched his brow, and his gaze dropped to their hands. "Should I kill him?" he asked, the offer putting the first genuine smile on Olivia's face since she'd woken up.

"Tempting," she said around a laugh, "but he's not worth the bullet."

"I can sick John Andre on him." At his name, John Andre ran into the kitchen, small bone barely sticking out each corner of his mouth, making him look like he was smiling. Dad bent and picked the small pup up. "Look at him. He's vicious."

This time Olivia laughed so hard she snorted, something she hadn't done in a long time. Daniel once commented on her snorting, and she'd become self-conscious. "He's just a natural born killer." John Andre's head tilted, his big brown eyes the epitome of innocence. Olivia moved in and kissed his snout. "You're just a big mean meanie, aren't you?" The bone fell from John Andre's mouth, and his tongue lapped out and swiped a wet line across Olivia's cheek. She laughed harder, and John Andre did his doggie dance in Dad's arms before Olivia took him in hers. He continued to attack her face with puppy kisses, and normally Olivia would freak out about her makeup, but today she took comfort in the affection.

Maybe moving back home, for now, wasn't so bad after all.

chapter 5

Shane spent his morning getting to know Mimi. But mainly he spoke about himself. Every time he had tried to steer the conversation to the family—or more importantly, his father—Mimi brought the subject back to him. With little to no information from Mimi, he'd hoped he'd get to meet his grandfather, but the man was MIA. According to Mimi, he was extremely busy with work, and Shane would get the chance to meet him very soon. She sounded optimistic, but Shane wasn't.

He wanted to believe her, especially since the man had to have been a hard worker to acquire his wealth, but something in the back of Shane's mind made him think work had nothing to do with his grandfather's absence.

After all, there had to be a reason Mom hid this part of his family from him. What weren't they telling him? He hoped he was overthinking, looking for the worst-case scenario, but his entire life was filled with curve balls and disappointment. He wasn't ready to believe that now he'd found the people where his bloodline originated that everything was going to be okay.

Mimi had hugged him at least four times before he was finally able to leave the house and make his way to McConnell Pub. He'd been pleasantly surprised by how easily Mimi and Uncle Grady had accepted him. He only hoped that pattern continued when he met his cousin.

He walked down Main Street toward the pub. He regretted selling his car now, but it was either that or have Mimi pay his way, and that hadn't been an option.

Fifteen minutes later, he reached the pub and headed inside. Embossed tin lined the ceiling, and a brick wall that looked original to the building sat behind the polished wood bar that was fully stocked with hundreds of bottles of liquor. High-back stools with black leather seats were mostly empty except for a man at the far end who turned as soon as he entered.

"Hey there," the man said. His long black hair was pulled into a ponytail, and the fine lines around his eyes put him in his late-forties, early fifties.

Shane nodded.

"New to town?" the man asked before Shane could manage a word. He was starting to think he had a sticker on his forehead that said, *I'm new here. Ask me about it.*

"I am. I'm actually looking for Connor."

"He had to run down to The Book Nook to drop Jean's lunch off. He should be back in a few minutes."

"Does he always leave the place unattended?" As far as Shane could tell, there were no other workers in the building, and the man was in the middle of eating a burger and drinking a beer, which made Shane think he was a customer not an employee.

"Oh yeah. I told him I'd hold the fort down until he returned." The man wiped his palm on his pant leg then held his hand out to Shane. "I'm Hal."

The name sounded familiar, and as Shane walked toward the man to shake his hand, he remembered Olivia and Milo's conversation from the night before. "You're the Alice Cooper impersonator?"

A big grin crossed his face. "Have you seen one of my shows?"

"I haven't been so lucky," he said. "Friends of mine told me about you. Said you're a must-see talent."

His lip tugged hard to the right but never fully formed, like he was trying to remain modest. "I'm playing here tonight. You should check out the show."

"I'll do that," Shane said.

The door opened, and Hal pointed to the door. "And here he is."

Shane turned, and Connor walked in; a close-trimmed beard like Shane's surrounded a welcoming smile. His dark hair was cut short on the sides but longer in the front, and his eyes were green just like his father's.

"You must be my long-lost cousin," Connor said, taking his hand and instantly pulling him in for a hug. Connor patted his back and pulled away. "Nice to meet you, man."

"Yeah, nice to meet you, too." Shane tried to hide the shock in his tone. It's not like he had expected Connor to have tossed his ass out on the pavement, but he didn't expect the friendly embrace either. Though, after all of Mimi's hugs, he was starting to wonder if the McConnell's were just an affectionate family.

"Long lost cousin," Hal said. "Am I the first to find out

about this?" The excitement in his voice had Shane lifting an eyebrow.

"It hasn't hit the town gossip mill yet," Connor answered. "But I'm sure it's only a matter of how long it takes you to finish that beer."

Hal picked up the pint glass and downed the rest of its contents. He grabbed the half-eaten burger and got up from the stool. "Wait till I tell Jean about this." Hal hurried out the door, burger in hand, while Shane stared after him.

"I hope he paid," Shane finally said, and Connor laughed.

"He helped me restock the bar today, so lunch was on the house."

"Does he work here?"

"Sometimes," Connor said. "My dad said you were looking for a job."

"I am. Mimi has been gracious enough to give me a place to stay, but I need to work. I don't like to sit around, and I like to have my own income."

Connor walked around the bar and grabbed a glass. "I respect that. It's pretty much the McConnell way, so there's no denying you're one of us. You want a drink?"

"No drink; just a job."

Connor filled the glass with water and took a sip. "You ever work in a pub before?"

"For about six months." He had quit when Mom had gotten sick, so he could spend more time with her. Looking back, he was grateful for that time he had with her and even more grateful that he had started working and saving as soon as he was old enough to do so.

"So, you know the basics."

"Pretty much, and I'm a fast learner, so I should quickly pick up what I don't know."

"Another McConnell trait."

It was weird to hear someone tell Shane his traits were related to a bloodline he knew so little about. He'd always thought his drive to work and keep busy came from Mom who had been as stubborn as she was determined. But maybe the blood that ran through him was more significant than he ever imagined.

Mom had always said he was just like his father, but he assumed she was only trying to give Shane some sort of connection to the man who helped create him and who he'd never gotten the chance to know. Maybe Mom had been telling him the truth all along.

The thought gave him a sense of belonging, something he hadn't felt since Mom passed. He swallowed down the unexpected emotion that thought filled him with and forced his attention back to his cousin. "When can I start?" He wasn't going to beat around the bush. He needed a job, and if Connor wasn't going to hire him, there was no use wasting any more time.

"How about now?"

"Now?" Shane glanced around the empty pub. "There's no one here."

"Not yet," Connor said. "But at about twelve-thirty Antonio and Maria will close up Shear Heaven for an hour lunch break and stop in and order the lunch special, which is a cup of our famous white chili and a slice of our homemade Irish soda bread. Then at twelve-forty-five the Amato Construction crew will be in for burgers. Once the high school lets out, we'll have a rush of rowdy teenagers who love their Coke and mozzarella sticks. Then it's a constant flow of customers until Hal takes the stage at eight. Then it's mainly drink orders and half-off appetizers until close."

"What time you close?"

"Weekdays nine, weekends eleven… until tourist season hits Then one in the morning."

With hours like that, it would help keep him busy. He'd take as many shifts as he could and save the money while he was currently rent free. He still wasn't sure how long he was staying in Morgan's Bay, though Mimi assured him the invitation was open for as long as he'd like. He had nowhere else to go, so it would make sense to stay, but he didn't want to depend on their hospitality for too long.

The house he was staying in was a rental, which meant the longer he stayed, the longer they were losing income. Not that he imagined the income one rental would generate would even hurt them, especially when they practically owned the entire town. Olivia had been right about that. He smiled thinking about the hot mess he met on the train. Bumping into her was another reason why he wasn't in a rush to leave just yet. He wouldn't mind being her rebound and having a little fun. He'd give it a couple weeks and reevaluate from there.

"So, what do you say?"

He held his hand out to Connor. "Let's do this."

***

McConnell's Pub had been the scene of many breakup conversations, and today was no different. Olivia sat in a booth across from her two best friends, Harper and Isla, filling them in on everything that went down the night before, including her encounter with the mysterious new McConnell.

She'd spent a good portion of her night reliving the car ride, trying to recall everything she'd said. Once the shock wore off after realizing Shane was a McConnell, she was left confused but mostly annoyed. She and Milo had gone on and on about his family; why hadn't he stopped her? Especially when he had said he didn't want someone else's opinion of his family to affect his initial impression. If that were the case, then he failed miserably. There wasn't much she and Milo didn't say.

It wasn't just the embarrassment, though. When his eyes met hers right before his big reveal, there'd been a spark that set her soul on fire. For that blip of a second, Daniel didn't exist; the heartache and anger that had raged inside her subsided, giving way to a light she couldn't ignore.

"Another McConnell, huh?" Harper said, tapping a finger stained with orange paint to her chin. She had just come from a paint party at the senior center where she'd taught the seniors how to paint a sunset.

Isla laughed. "Don't get any ideas, Harp. I'm pretty sure Olivia has already staked her claim."

"Daniel and I just broke up yesterday. I'm not staking claim on anyone."

Harper nodded over Olivia's shoulder. "Then you wouldn't mind if I went over and talked to him?"

Olivia's eyes widened, and she spun on her chair following the direction of Harper's gaze. Behind the bar in all his masculine glory was Shane. His attention cut toward her, and she jolted around before they could make eye contact.

"That's him, right?" Harper asked.

"Yup." Olivia leaned back in her chair. "How did you know?"

"Lucky guess."

Isla rolled her aquamarine eyes. "Lucky guess, my butt. What are the chances there are two new guys in town? There was no luck involved."

Harper sighed, disappointment drooping her shoulders. "Either way, by Liv's reaction, it's obvious he's off the market."

"I just told you, I'm getting over Daniel. I'm not going to jump back into dating, especially with a guy I know nothing about. Besides, I'm sure he'd want nothing to do with me. I told you how crazy I was on the train."

"Yes." Isla took a sip of her sangria. "But you also told us how good looking he was, how sweet he was to carry your bag and get it out of the trunk, and how your eyes locked and fireworks went off right before he dropped the bomb."

"That's not what I said."

"I'm paraphrasing, but that's basically everything you said."

Olivia wasn't going to argue. Nobody won an argument

against Isla, even if they were right. Olivia wanted to look over her shoulder and get another glimpse. She was annoyed at herself for sitting with her back to the bar. "How did I not realize he was here?"

"I noticed," Harper said. "He's nice to look at."

"Then why didn't you say anything?"

Harper shrugged. "I wanted ten minutes to fantasize that he wasn't your Shane, I'd get a chance, and finally be able to give up online dating."

"Milo said you had a date last night. I'm guessing it didn't go well."

Harper's head fell forward, and her shoulders shook with miserable laughter. "He wanted to share an entrée, so he only had to pay a sharing fee instead of full price for two dinners."

"Cheap bastard!" Isla exclaimed. "I hope you walked out right then and there."

Harper downed the rest of her margarita. "I stayed and paid for my own meal."

Isla's eyes doubled in size. "Harper! You deserve better than that."

"I was starving, and the restaurant had good ratings. I didn't know when I'd ever go back there, so I stayed for the food."

"Was it worth it?" Isla asked.

"Oh yeah."

Olivia zoned out of their conversation; her mind too focused on the guy behind the bar. After a few minutes, she grabbed Harper's empty glass. "Want another one?"

Before Harper could answer, Olivia was already on her way to the bar. Shane stood at the far end, getting a drink for Mr. Peterson. Olivia leaned against the bar, trying not to stare. She placed the empty glass on the bar top and waited as if this were any other day.

Shane handed Mr. Peterson his drink and tossed a dish rag over his shoulder. He turned, his eyes immediately landing on Olivia. Heat trickled through her body from the intent in his stare. He moved toward her with an ease that was both confident and laidback. He propped himself against the bar directly across from her. The muscles of his arms pressed nicely against his short black sleeves.

"Are you stalking me?" he asked, eyebrow raised in an intriguing, yet very attractive way.

Olivia played it as coy as possible. "No, McConnell's has the best burgers."

He rubbed his chin and laughed. "I remember you saying that on your tour."

She bit her lip, eyes drifting down to the shiny wood of the bar before she found the courage to look him in the eye. "About that… Why didn't you stop me? Tell me who you really were?" She felt like such an idiot, then toss in all the stuff Milo had said about her obsession with the McConnell's, and she was downright embarrassed.

"I guess I didn't want you to judge me before you got to know me."

The sincerity in his tone matched the honesty in his gaze, and though she was still slightly embarrassed, she understood. "I just feel bad that I might have influenced your first impression of your family."

"You did."

Guilt tied her stomach in knots. "I'm sorry."

"It wasn't a bad thing. I was expecting rich snobs, but I was met with the total opposite. Mimi was warm and accepting. My uncle was kind and willing to help me out, no questions asked. I was afraid I'd be met with opposition, but they welcomed with me with open arms. And so did Connor. It's crazy. The only family I've ever known is my mom, and now I have this whole new family that, up until a few weeks ago, I had no idea existed."

He didn't smile, but he didn't have to, she could hear the relief in his tone. "I'm happy it worked out. Everybody deserves the love of family."

"Thanks." He nodded toward the empty glass. "Another margarita for your friend."

"How do you know it's not for me?"

"You're drinking Cabernet Sauvignon."

Intrigued, she smiled. "You pay attention to detail." It was something Daniel never did. As if it would kill the guy to remember their anniversary. She supposed it was a date he didn't *want* to remember.

She shook the annoyed anger from her mind, forgetting about the two-timing jerk, and focused on Shane. "Another margarita for my friend, and I'll take another Cabernet."

"Coming right up."

She watched as he moved effortlessly behind the bar. "Is this a permanent gig or just helping Connor out?"

"I'm not sure. I don't like to look too far into the

future." He walked over to her and placed the two drinks on the bar in front of her. "Prefer to take one day at a time."

"How's that margarita going?" Harper called from the table, and Olivia laughed.

"I should get back."

"Of course."

She took the two drinks in her hand. "If you get a break, stop by the table and meet the girls. If you're going to be bartending here, you might as well get to know the regulars."

He smiled. "I'll do that."

Olivia headed to the table, fighting with her lips to stay flat and indifferent, but as soon as she sat down her mouth betrayed her. Her lips curved upward, and her cheeks filled with heat, most likely turning them a horrible shade of red.

She handed Harper her drink, and Harper sighed.

"Yup, he's definitely out of the question."

<h1 style="text-align:center">chapter 6</h1>

Olivia checked the fridge for the nine hundredth time. Both her parents were at work, and John Andre was settled on the couch for his afternoon nap. She'd call Isla or Harper, but Isla was working the register at her parents' florist shop, and Harper was doing another paint event at the library. Olivia was unemployed and bored. And hungry. Her stomach growled at that moment as if agreeing with her.

Every time she opened the fridge, she'd hoped something new would appear, but it was still exactly the same. Eggs, milk, leftovers from God only knows when, and a tub of sour cream—no fresh fruit or vegetables from the farmer's market, no Greek yogurt or artisanal cheese to snack on.

"Forget this," Olivia announced, and John Andre didn't even poke his head up from his perch. She grabbed her purse and headed out. A cheat day was calling out to her, and a burger from McConnell's Pub sounded like the perfect remedy to her growling stomach. Also, she wouldn't mind a little conversation with someone who wasn't an eight-pound walking ball of fur. Connor was always a good conversationalist… or Shane.

It's not like she was going to McConnell's just to see him. So what if he was a beautiful specimen of a man, and he'd carried her bags for her, met her eyes when he spoke like he was talking to her and not down or over her? She wasn't going for him. She was going for a burger.

She made herself believe the lie the entire way to the front door when she realized she wasn't in Manhattan. She couldn't step outside and wave down a cab. She couldn't call a car service or hop on the nearest subway. She was in Morgan's Bay, where a car was essential.

"Damn it," she mumbled under her breath, and her stomach joined the chorus with a loud rumble. She looked down at the strappy three-inch heels she'd paired with her black shorts and three quarter-sleeve white top. Not exactly the best outfit to walk the mile to Main Street.

There was only one option, and she did not want to sink to such levels, but she was hungry and in desperate need of social interaction. She turned back and grabbed the keys to her parents' golf cart—the same cart Olivia was embarrassed of the minute her parents bought it and explained it was to put-put around the neighborhood. According to them, John Andre liked the wind in his face. Olivia liked to roll down a window on a nice summer day, too, but her parents didn't run out and buy her a golf cart.

She tossed all the ill-will to the back of her mind and headed to the garage. She'd never driven the blasted thing, but it couldn't be that hard. She found the ignition, stuck the key in, and turned it over.

The cart sputtered to life and Olivia placed her bag on the seat beside her. She pushed down on the gas, and the cart moved forward. Dad wasn't kidding when he said to put-put around the neighborhood; this thing couldn't get out of its own way. At this rate, she'd be better off walking, but then she thought of the potential blisters and pressed down on the pedal, hoping the golf cart would find some will to speed up.

It didn't.

Olivia pressed on. She focused on the cheeseburger, but Shane's face quickly overpowered that vision. A smile came to her face when she thought of their interaction the other night. He was not only easy to talk to when she wasn't a blubbering mess, but he also paid attention to the little things. Daniel couldn't even remember her birthday.

She continued on her way to Main Street when she did a double take at the triangular figure walking down the street. If she was in the city, she would have kept going without even a glance in the oddity's direction, but this wasn't the city.

She slowed the golf cart, and as she approached the triangle turned, revealing it was actually a life-size costume of a slice of pizza, and Hal's head popped through a pepperoni circle at the top. His long black hair must've been pulled back.

While Olivia should've been surprised, she wasn't. It was Hal after all.

"Olivia!" Hal's arms came up, big white, Mickey-Mouse-looking gloves on each hand. "It's so good to see you."

"Hal." She stopped, trying to find the words as she took in the triangular costume, complete with a pair of ridiculously oversized cartoon-like sneakers. "You're a slice of pizza.”

“Got a job at Carlos’ handing out flyers. I’m on my way there now.”

“Where’s your van?” she asked. He had a big black van that would be suspicious driving down any area with children, but the only thing Hal kept in the back was his guitar amp.

“In the shop. The AC went, and I figured I should get it fixed before the humidity rolls in.”

“Hop in. I’ll give you a ride.”

“You always were a sweet girl.” He lifted one bulky sneaker that reminded Olivia of her dad’s monster slippers into the cart. He lifted himself up and turned to sit. He bent down adjusting his costume, the top of the crust knocking Olivia’s sunglasses off her face.

After much movement, Hal settled and Olivia fixed her glasses. “We good?” she asked, and he nodded. Olivia hit the gas and continued on. “How’s the music going?” Her gaze drifted to Hal, and his face lit up.

“Great! I’ll be playing at Greta’s tonight. You and the fam should stop by.”

“I’ll see if my parents are up to it.”

He held out a flyer, and she took it. One hand on the wheel, she glanced at the paper.

“On the front is a coupon for Carlos’. You get a dozen garlic knots on the house, and on the back…” Hal waited for Olivia to turn the flyer over. She bit her lip to keep from laughing. There was a closeup picture of Hal decked out in his Alice Cooper makeup, tongue out, fingers bent in the rock and roll devil horn symbol.

"I'll save this for later." She held the steering wheel with her elbows and made a show of folding the flyer and tucking it safely in her purse.

She talked with Hal, mainly about his music, until they reached their final destination. Hal jumped out first, his costume getting stuck on the frame of the cart. Olivia gave it a good shove, and Hal popped free.

"Thanks for the ride," he said. "Hope to see you tonight."

Olivia waved, a familiar calm coming over her. She acted like she hated small town life and she was a city girl at heart, but a simple conversation with Hal had made her feel more at home than she had in a while.

Olivia's phone vibrated, reverberating in her bag. She fished it out, and her heart dropped at Daniel's name flashing on her screen. Her good mood instantly gone.

Ignoring the asshole would be the smart thing to do, but curiosity was a bitch unfortunately. She clicked the text open and rolled her eyes.

Everyone is asking for you. What am I supposed to say?

Her lip curled, and rage simmered inside her, taking over her fingers as she violently tapped a reply on the screen, wishing it was Daniel's face.

You can tell them that you're a no good, two timing jerk who used me in your climb to the top.

Unbelievable. He cheated on her, and now he expected her to bail his ass out. It wasn't going to happen. It wasn't her fault he couldn't keep Mr. Willy in his pants, and it sure as hell wasn't her fault that they were in this situation.

Her phone vibrated again, and she resisted the urge to chuck her phone in the street and watch as the next car drove by, crushing it into oblivion.

She gritted her teeth and opened the text.

Stop acting like a child.

She might've been twenty-five and unsure about most things in her life, but one fact remained true—she was not a child.

But if he thought she was, well than that's exactly what she was going to be. She had nothing to prove to him anymore. She picked her phone back up and shot off another text.

Excuse me I'm late for my playdate.

She hit send and shoved her phone in her bag. Victory consumed her for about two seconds, but that word kept flashing in her mind. *Child.*

Miles away and broken up, Daniel still managed to bring out her insecurities.

***

It'd been three days since Shane rolled into town, and he had yet to meet his grandfather. He wasn't delusional; he didn't expect the man to meet him at the train station with wide open arms, but he at least expected him to make an effort to meet the grandson he'd never met. He felt like an idiot every time he glanced toward the pub door, as if the man would pop in.

He didn't want to care, but the lack of interest ate at him. It made him question what sort of relationship his father must've had with the man. He'd accepted that he didn't have a father, and that was okay. He didn't know the man, so it's not like he ever had to feel the loss. Now, being in his father's hometown, he couldn't ignore the ache in his heart for a relationship that never was. And maybe that's why he was so disappointed. Maybe a part of him was hoping to bridge a gap in his life he didn't even know was there.

Connor reappeared from the kitchen and dropped a plate of nachos off at a table of older women who all held a copy of the same book in one hand and margaritas in the other. According to Connor, they met every Monday for book club, but their book club was really an excuse to day drink.

He made his way back and leaned against the bar. Humor lit the strong angles of Connor's face and glowed in his green eyes. "Make sure you keep the margaritas flowing for that group, or they'll get rowdy."

"Will do."

Shane glanced toward the door then at Connor. "Does our grandfather ever stop in?"

"Here?" Connor barked out a laugh and shook his head. "Even if pigs took flight down Main Street, he wouldn't come in here."

"I just thought…"

"That we were a close-knit family? No. We all just live in the same town. To be honest, if it wasn't for Mimi, we probably wouldn't even see each other."

"Oh." A strange disappointment settled in his stomach.

"Grandfather spends most of his time at his Manhattan office. He comes home Thursday night then heads out Sunday. Unless it's summer. Then he spends most of his days in his office at Bayview. Mimi can coax him out for a family dinner or an event."

"Are you two close?"

"Depends on your definition of close. I see him on occasion, and we talk about the Yankees. He has season tickets on the front baseline. He usually uses them to schmooze clients, but every now and again he'll offer me a ticket." Connor tapped Shane's shoulder. "Hey, maybe we'll get to go this summer. Watch a few innings, throw back a few beers."

"Sounds great." Shane had only been to one baseball game his whole life—the Angels vs the Mariners. His mom had gotten them tickets when she'd gotten a raise because he had always wanted to go. She'd always been selfless like that—always doing everything for him and nothing for herself. She was so busy taking care of him she didn't even realize when her own health had declined.

Visions of her emaciated in a hospital bed filtered into his mind. He swallowed hard and shook his head. He wasn't going back there. Not now.

"So, does that mean you might be sticking around for a while?"

Shane didn't want to commit, but he also didn't want to let Connor down. "It's a possibility. Not like I have anywhere else to go."

"I know you said it was just you and your mom, but do

you not have any other family?"

Shane shook his head. "Nope."

"Our family might be a bit dysfunctional, and we might not be the family you dreamed about, but we're yours now."

It was more than Shane had, and though he was hesitant to step into and accept this new family as his own, he was grateful to Connor for welcoming him so easily. "I appreciate that."

"We don't have to hug now or anything, right?" Connor asked.

Shane's eyebrow arched, and he leaned back. "I sure as hell hope not."

Connor gave him a knowing smile. "You'll fit in just fine."

The door opened, and out of habit, Shane's attention went to the entrance. Olivia appeared, the sunlight encircling her as if she were a walking beam of light. His gaze immediately dropped to the long curve of her bare legs before roaming up and settling on her deep brown eyes.

"Looks like family's not the only reason for you to stay." Connor patted Shane's back and disappeared into the kitchen. He was about to make a joke when he saw the array of emotions fighting for the spotlight on Olivia's face.

"Rough day?" he asked as she approached the bar.

She dropped her bag on the top of the bar and hopped onto the barstool, slouching on the bar top. "Are all men assholes or just a select few? Is it like a gene or something?"

"Boyfriend trouble?" he asked.

Her lip curled in disgust. "*Ex*-boyfriend. And kind of."

"Want to talk about it?"

"Not really."

"Okay then what can I get—?"

"It's just that we were together for a long time, and you would think I would have noticed I was dating a total jerk. But no, I was blissfully unaware of the magnitude of douchebag that was contained in that custom suit of his."

Shane rested his arms on the bar beside her and leaned forward. "Maybe you didn't want to see it." She blinked up, brown eyes like deep pools of chocolate he'd be more than happy to drown in for a night. "Sometimes it's easier to pretend everything's okay rather than accepting that it's not."

He'd done it all too often. First when he was sick, refusing to accept his diagnosis. Then when Mom got sick. Denial was a better state of mind… until it wasn't.

"I guess you could be right. Look at me now. I had to do my own blowout this morning." She made a sweeping motion toward her hair. "I'm homeless, jobless, and an emotional train wreck."

Shane shook his head and laughed. "No, the other night you were an emotional train wreck. Today you seem like you're on your way to figuring out your next steps without him in your life."

Her glossed lips pressed together in what looked like an attempt to hide a smile. He wished she didn't suppress it. Her smile was beautiful. "I hope so. Right now, I feel like I'm never going to figure out my next step."

He rested a comforting hand on hers; an unexpected jolt of electricity shot through his arm and right to his groin.

He swallowed down the rise of desire the touch of her skin against his awakened inside him and focused on the conversation.

"You will," he said.

"How do you know?"

A smirk pulled at the corner of his mouth. "Because there's a fire in you. I saw it the first time I met you, and I can see it now, and that fire is not something that can be contained." He felt it when he touched her, too. Heat roared beneath the surface, begging to be released. He wouldn't mind helping her free the built-up inferno for a night. He'd bet money that one seductive touch to her prissy demeanor would spark a blaze of passion inside her, making her become overzealous and eager to take him.

"You're good at this," she said.

His brow furrowed, knocking him away from visions of Olivia satiated and naked beneath him. "And what's that?"

"Being a bartender."

"I haven't even offered you a drink."

"No, but a good bartender is much more than the drinks they make. A good bartender knows how to talk to people, and a good bartender knows exactly what to say to make their train wreck of a customer have hope again."

"I'm happy I could help. Now back to the other portion of being a good bartender. What can I get you? A burger?"

Her head tilted, and her hair fell forward and brushed against her cheek. "How do you know I'm going to order a burger?" She pushed the chestnut strands behind a delicate ear.

"You look like you need a cheat day." He wrote down her order. "Besides, why would you order anything else other than the best?"

Her eyes dropped to the bar, and a sadness surrounded her, sagging her shoulders and frowning.

"Hey, you okay?" Shane asked. He didn't mean to upset the girl. If she didn't want to commit to a cheat day, he'd get her a kale salad or whatever it was she ate.

She glanced up, a forced smile on her face. "It's silly really."

"I like silly. Tell me."

She bit her lip as if she was debating whether to tell him or not. An air of shyness floated around her. He waited, hoping she'd let him in on whatever she was thinking. Normally, he wouldn't care, but he wanted to know what went through her head.

"It's just that I've known you for what? Three days? And I feel like you already know me better and understand me better than my ex ever did."

The honesty was a shock to his system, but her words warmed him unexpectedly, and pride swelled in his chest. "When a pretty girl talks, I listen." He might've steered clear of relationships, but he knew how to give women exactly what they wanted.

Disappointment tugged at the corners of her eyes, but she pressed her lips upward anyway. "Damn, and here I thought I was special."

He reached across the bar, taking her hand in his to add

weight to his words, but mainly because he wanted to feel the softness of her hand against his again. He ran the pad of his thumb across her knuckle and met her eyes, holding her gaze for a quiet moment. "You are."

The disappointment vanished from her features as a pretty blush crept up her neck and into her cheeks.

Satisfied with her reaction, he let go of her hand. "How about that burger?"

"How about more margaritas!" The table of margarita drinking women all held their drinks up in solidarity.

Olivia covered her mouth and muffled a laugh. "You better get on that before they get rowdy. Hi ladies," Olivia waved then turned back to Shane. "I'll keep them in line while you get started on those margaritas." She slid off the stool and strutted toward the women.

Shane watched as she greeted each of the book club members then with confident ease, rested her hand on the back of a chair to continue the conversation.

In the way she dressed and carried herself, Olivia came across as confident, but Shane could see beyond the façade. He could see the insecurities and uncertainties that poked beneath the surface, but as he watched her speak to the table of women, those nuances of self-doubt vanished.

Shane prepared a pitcher of margaritas for the table and passed off Olivia's order to Connor. It'd been only a couple days, but he already felt like he belonged, manning the bar and working as a team with his cousin. He grabbed the pitcher and brought it over to the table. He was greeted with cheers as he filled all the glasses.

"I'll let you ladies get back to your discussion," Olivia said.

The woman with the black rimmed glasses and salt and pepper shoulder-length hair patted Olivia's hand and looked at her with warm affection. "Don't forget to stop by. I'll find you something to combat the boredom."

"Will do."

Olivia followed Shane to the bar and slid onto her stool.

Shane nodded to the table. "Thanks for your help."

Olivia waved his appreciation away. "It was nothing. I've known every single one of those women my entire life. And it worked out for me since I got the welcome back greetings done in one fell swoop."

"In that case, you're welcome."

Olivia laughed under her breath, shaking her head as amusement danced in her eyes.

"Connor said they come in here every Monday for book club," Shane said.

"It's really the margarita club with a side of reading."

Shane rubbed at his chin. "Connor said something along those lines, too."

"They're all really good people though." Olivia turned her body slightly to face the women. "Strap in. I'm about to give you a crash course." She nodded to the table. "The lady with the glasses that has a Diane Keaton vibe, that's Jean Kelly. She owns The Book Nook. You answer a few questions, and she will find you the perfect book. Her husband passed away when I was eleven.

The whole town mourned with her and their two kids who are well into their thirties now. Mr. Kelly was one of the good ones." Olivia was quiet for a moment before continuing. "Next to Jean is Maria. She owns the hair salon Shear Heaven with her husband, Antonio. Well, it's split up into a barbershop/salon. I used to babysit their daughter Sofia when I was in high school. Next to Maria is Miss Karen. She owns Pie in the Sky where you will have the best pie you've ever had in your entire life. I have to limit myself when I'm home, or I'd be in there every single day it's that good."

"Does she have coconut cream?"

An adorable smirk quirked at the edge of her lips. "Is that your favorite?"

"Possibly."

"Then you are in for a treat. Tell you what... I'll buy your first slice. She closes early on Mondays for book club, so what about tomorrow morning? Say ten?"

"Are you asking me out?" Shane asked with a flirtatious tone. Since she just broke up with her ex, there was no chance she'd get attached. It was a win-win for both of them. He could help her move on and have some fun while he was in town.

Olivia's teeth slid over her lip. "I'm asking you to join me for a once-in-a-lifetime experience. But if you're not up to the challenge..."

"Oh, I'm definitely up for it. I just wanted to know if kissing you afterward would be bad form."

Her eyes widened at his bluntness, but luckily for him,

she didn't look too upset by the suggestion. If anything, she looked flattered.

Shane usually avoided romantic entanglements. Everyone he'd ever loved had died, and he had no idea what his expiration date was. He'd managed to prolong his several times, but he knew it was only a matter of time before he couldn't dodge the inevitable. Still, he was in a place he never expected to be, and there was nothing wrong with having a little fun.

"I don't know. If you remember our disastrous first meeting, I was heartbroken over a very recent breakup."

"You weren't that heartbroken," he said. Though, the fact that she'd recently got out of a relationship was exactly why he was pursuing this. She needed time to heal, to recover from the last guy, and he was willing to step in as her rebound.

"I love how you think you know me so well."

"I don't," he said. "I'd like to, though."

"Hypothetically speaking, if you were to kiss me after pie, I wouldn't turn my cheek to you."

"Good to know." He motioned toward the table. "Now let's get back to Morgan's Bay town directory. Who is the older woman with the bright pink hair?"

Olivia smiled, and this time let it spread wide across her face. A spark brightened her eyes. "That is Lillian, the coolest person you'll ever meet." Shane eyed her with doubt. "No honestly. I wanted to be her when I grew up."

"Why's that?"

"Her store, Lillian's closet, is my favorite place on earth.

I used to spend all my time there in high school."

"Is it like a clothing store?"

"'Is it like a clothing store?'" Olivia mocked. "It is so much more than that! Lillian opened the store back in the early 2000's when she decided to clean out her closet."

"She had that many clothes?"

"You have no idea. The racks were packed with designer pieces. As she'd sell and free up space, she'd just go to her stockpile and add more. Now she goes to estate and yard sales to buy clothes to keep her stock up. But when she first opened, I was eight, and I'd go with my mom and try on all the costume jewelry and carry around the designer bags. I always said to myself, one day I'd have a collection of fancy handbags."

"And do you."

"I'm still working on it." Olivia held up her checkered purse. "This is my first. One day I'll have more."

"Why bags? I mean what's so special about them?"

She shrugged. "I guess they always meant sophistication and femininity—two things I always wanted."

"From an outsider looking in, you don't need a bag to be either of those things. You're doing just fine on your own."

Her thick eyelashes brushed the apple of her cheeks before her eyes popped open and pinned him in place with a sultry stare. "You're just trying to seal the deal on that kiss."

"Hadn't crossed my mind, but if it's helping, I'll take the assist."

"It's helping," she admitted just as Connor brought out

her burger and ruined the moment. If that wasn't what family was for…

chapter 7

Olivia enjoyed her burger while Shane went to refill the book club's drinks. She held her glass of water up—she had a golf cart to operate after all—and toasted them. Lillian dodged her head around Shane, pointed at his butt, and gave Olivia a thumbs up. Olivia choked on her water.

Shane returned to his place behind the bar. He'd only been bartending for a couple days, yet the ease in which he moved and the confident way he carried a conversation… it was as if he'd been a part of the town for much longer.

"Those women can drink." He grabbed a lime and a knife, getting to work on refilling the condiment tray.

Olivia popped a fry in her mouth and chewed. "Oh, that's nothing. Wait until after the Memorial Day parade."

His hand stilled in mid slice. Her eyes roamed the long length of his fingers, and instant heat bloomed in her cheeks when her mind took her to an X-rated feature.

"Parade?"

She shook away the sexy thoughts and brought her attention to the confused look in his eyes. "What, they don't have those where you come from?"

"They probably did, but I've never been to one. I've watched the Macy's Thanksgiving Day Parade on television."

"Oh, that parade is a masterpiece compared to any of the Morgan's Bay parades. Most of the spectators come out to see what's going to go wrong. Last year, Mr. Clifford's dog jumped out of his classic Buick convertible and ate the ice cream right out of little Lily Cain's cone. And the year before that, Miss Katy's Daisy Troop was handing out red, white, and blue beaded necklaces when one of the girls decided she didn't want to anymore, so she threw her stash on the ground and kept walking."

"That's not too bad."

"It wasn't until the school marching band came through, and an unsuspecting flag tosser face planted, causing a domino effect throughout the brass section."

"Ouch."

"That year we made more than the local news." When she went back to work, more than one person had asked if she was there. She'd been front row to the mayhem and recounted the entire mishap again and again. "Our little town was famous for a day."

"Interesting."

"What's that?" she asked.

He rested his hands on either side of the bar and leaned forward. She swallowed at how close that move brought him to her. If it wasn't for the bar between them, she'd be able to feel the heat from his body. She swallowed, thinking about what it would be like to feel his hands on her body, his lips moving across hers with passion fueled desire.

If he wasn't kidding earlier, there was a possibility she'd find out. The thought both thrilled her and terrified her. She hadn't kissed anyone other than Daniel in over three years. What if their styles weren't compatible? What if he thought she was a terrible kisser?

His greener eyes—thanks to his green shirt— focused on her. She cleared her mind of all the ways his lips could move against hers. "What's interesting?" she asked, her words soft and breathy.

"When I first met you, I assumed you were this city girl, but you're not, are you?"

"Of course I am. I've lived in the city since my first semester of college." As soon as she got off the train at Penn Station it was like she was finally home. She always felt held back living in a small town, and she didn't feel that way in the city. She felt wild and free, reckless and unrestricted, able to do whatever she pleased without the rumor mill making it back to her parents.

More than anything, she felt alive—the energy of walking through Midtown, the calm of strolling through Central Park, and the elegance of the Upper East Side, knowing she got to call all of it home.

"Lived there, yes, but your heart, it never left here. I can tell by the way you talk about this place. You get this glint in your eyes and this adorable smile."

"It's funny. I was just thinking about this on the way here in my parents' golf cart. My whole life all I ever wanted was to be a city girl. But it was nice to see Hal on my way here and be able to stop and offer him a ride. That's something you don't get in the city. People are too consumed in their lives to stop and chat. I guess I missed that."

Shane held his hands up, lips parted ever so slightly, a

befuddled look on his handsome face. "I'm sorry, you lost me at golf cart."

"I just had a touching revelation, and all you got out of that was I drove here in a golf cart."

"It was kind of a banana ball."

The skin above her nose pinched in confusion. "A what?"

"A little golf humor."

"Wait… did you just hit me with a dad joke?"

"It wasn't a dad joke. It was golf humor."

"A dad joke disguised as golf humor." Olivia laughed.

"Go ahead make fun of me. But remember you're the one who drove here in a golf cart."

Olivia held up a fry and pointed it at Shane. "Touché." She pushed the plate away and slumped against the high back of the stool.

"Done?" Shane asked.

"Yes. If I eat another fry, I might not fit in the golf cart."

She reached into her purse, grabbed her wallet, and handed over her Amex. He took it from her, his finger brushing gently against hers. Sparks ignited at his touch and traveled up her arm in an explosion of heat. A tiny gasp escaped her, and she cleared her throat to try and cover it up.

Shane took her card, seeming unaware of the things his touch had done to her body. He went to the credit card machine and swiped. Olivia took the second his back was to her to take a breath.

He returned with the card and slowly slid it across the

bar.

She picked it up looking for the receipt to sign, but all he gave her was the card. "Don't I have to sign the receipt?"

"Don't worry about it."

Her eyebrows pinched in confusion. "I always sign when I come here."

His gaze casted downward. "Your card was declined."

"What?" Her eyes widened, and she shot off the bar stool. "What do you mean it was declined? Try it again."

"I put it through twice. Both times it was declined."

"That no good—" She stopped herself. Of course Daniel would cancel her credit card. It didn't matter that she paid the damn bill for it every month. If it wasn't for him, she never would have been able to get the card in the first place. When they started dating, she'd had no credit history. Her parents had taken out loans to pay for her schooling in their name and she never bought a car since she lived in the city.

She grabbed her phone, fingers ready to shoot off an angry text, but she stopped herself. It would only reinforce his stance on her acting like a child. She didn't need him or that stupid credit card. She could figure out how to pay her own way. Maybe she could wash dishes… but her manicure was already chipping...

Her eye caught on the strip of white paper Shane slyly—or so he thought—slid beneath the machine. She pointed toward the paper. "Wait. I saw a receipt come out."

His hand fell away, and he shrugged. "I put my own card through."

Olivia stared at him, trying to figure this man out. "Why would you do that?"

"I didn't want to embarrass you."

"Thank you. That was very sweet of you, but I'm going to pay you back."

"You paid for my ride the other night. Consider us even."

"What ride…oh. I was paying anyway." It would have been the same price whether Shane got in the car with her or not.

"We shared the ride; I should've paid my half."

"Okay, fine. We'll consider it even." She placed her card back in her wallet and checked the cash slot, but other than a few singles, it was sadly lacking. "So, about tomorrow… I might need a rain check."

"Oh no," Shane said. "You promised me the best pie I have ever eaten, and there is no way I'm going to miss out on that."

"But I don't have…" She couldn't even finish the sentence. Embarrassment prickled in her throat. How did she go from living in a penthouse apartment above one of the wealthiest neighborhoods in Manhattan to not even being able to afford a single slice of pie?

If she didn't clear her bank account out during that sale last week, she'd be able to buy Karen's entire day's inventory. Maybe Daniel was right… Maybe she was a child.

Shane tapped the bar, drawing her attention back to him. "I'm treating tomorrow, and I don't want to hear any arguments."

Guilt edged at her gut. She was the one who offered, and she felt silly that she couldn't hold up her end of the deal. "Are you sure?"

"Absolutely."

"Then it's still a date?"

The corner of his mouth quirked, creating an unexpected dimple. "It's still a date."

"I can't wait." She slid off the stool and adjusted her shorts. "In the meantime, I have to go try to figure out how to make some extra money while I'm home."

"Ever think about waitressing?" Shane asked.

"No, but I wouldn't be opposed to it." Harper waitressed for a few summers and made a killing in tips. At this rate she would take any source of income she could get, even if it meant putting her manicure at risk. "Why do you ask?"

"I heard Connor on the phone with someone about placing an ad in the local paper for another waitress. I can put in a good word for you."

"Technically, I've known Connor longer than you, but if you're offering, why not? It couldn't hurt."

"What about I go grab him, and you two can work it out."

"You wouldn't mind working with me?" Anticipation sat idly in her stomach while she waited for his response.

"Not only wouldn't I mind, I'm looking forward to it."

Heat crept into her cheeks, and she let her hair fall forward to conceal her face. Blotchy red had never been a good look on her. "In that case, go get him."

It wasn't a position in her field of marketing or social media, but until she figured out her next move, it was something to help pay the bills. She might even make enough in tips to head back to the city and get her hair and nails done at her favorite salon.

"I'll be right back." Shane offered her a wink, and she suppressed a giddy smile.

Three days ago, Olivia thought her world was coming to an end, but now the idea of working with Shane, spending time with him and getting to know him, suddenly her world seemed like it wasn't ending but starting anew.

chapter 8

Shane dressed in his usual shorts and t-shirt before heading out. It'd been a long time since he'd been on a date. He'd been more of a casual hook-up kind of guy since both people went in knowing it was only for the night. He had a strict rule about relationships, but since Olivia was currently bouncing back from one, she wouldn't be looking for anything serious from him. Besides, there was just something about her he couldn't resist.

What appealed to him most was her love for the town even if she claimed to be a city girl at heart. Chasing the cheapest rent never gave him a chance to stay anywhere long enough to establish a sense of home. Mom became home, and when she passed, he was in every way homeless.

Shane wanted what Olivia had. He wanted to know what it was like to have roots. Maybe he'd never get the father on the doorstep at nightfall in monster slippers. But a place to call his own, a place where he knew everyone and was accepted? That sounded nice, but it also scared the hell out of him.

There was a reason he avoided relationships. For so long he had been a burden, and he never wanted to force that on anyone again. It was safer to avoid entanglements—avoid the pain and suffering that came along with caring for someone.

When Mom died, the heartache was enough to ignore what she had told him about the family he didn't know existed. He had been mad at her, and not because she'd kept it from him, but because she told him. He was perfectly content going through life never knowing.

He'd had no intention of reaching out to Mimi, or any of the McConnells for that matter, but something in the back of his head kept nudging him to make the call.

Now here he was, walking down the fronts steps of the house, happy as shit to go eat some pie with Olivia. He needed to be careful and not allow her or anyone to break down his resolve. Connor was great, and Olivia…well she was amazing, and that was exactly why he needed to stay strong. He didn't want to see them hurt in the end.

A black SUV pulled up in front of the house, and Shane froze for a moment. He squinted, trying to see through the dark black tint, but it was impossible. He had no idea who it could be. As far as Shane knew, this house was vacant for the foreseeable future. Unless it was the old tenant coming back to get something they'd forgotten?

The back-passenger window rolled down, and a man with grayish white hair that framed the perimeter of his face appeared. His eyes were far from welcoming, and even though Shane had never seen them before, he knew exactly who they belonged to.

He'd seen pictures when he was at Bayview Estate, and despite that, it was all in his eyes. The man was a McConnell through and through, and not just any McConnell—he was the patriarch.

"Grandpa?" Shane said as he approached the waiting vehicle.

"Get in." It wasn't a question and his tone told Shane he had no other options but to obey. Shane walked around to the driver side, opened the door and slid into a cloud of expensive leather and overpriced aftershave.

The driver didn't acknowledge Shane as he put the SUV in drive. Shane looked at his grandfather, unsure of what to say or how to proceed. Sweat beaded on his forehead, and he shifted in his seat. He probably watched one too many mafia movies, but all he could think was he would never be seen again.

"Your grandmother tells me you're working down at the pub." His voice was rough but seasoned, and paired with his demeanor and expensive looking suit, it created the picture of a powerful money maker who was to be taken seriously.

"I am," Shane answered.

"You're a go-getter. It's a good quality in a man."

"I don't expect anyone to pay my way when I'm capable of earning my own income." He didn't want his grandfather to think he was here to freeload. He was here to get answers about his father not to milk the family fortune dry.

"Independent… like your father."

Shane straightened in his seat. Mom had told him his independence was a trait he inherited from the old man, but hearing it come from this man who had known his father from birth, the impact was different. It went right to his heart and squeezed, making him regret even more the time they never got together.

"What else was my father like?" Mimi had been a dead end, and Shane had almost given up hope, but now he might finally get the answers he was hoping for.

"A self-indulgent disappointment."

Shock smacked Shane across the face and ricocheted through his gut. "Geez Gramps, tell me how you really feel." No wonder Dad left and didn't look back. Shane didn't expect rainbows and sunshine from the man, but a proper introduction instead of going straight for the kill, would have been nice.

"Don't call me that," he stated dryly. "Your father had such promise, and he threw it all away on a one-way ticket to California."

Shane wanted to know about his father, but he had no intention of listening to his grandfather rip apart the man who wasn't even alive to defend himself. "I've known you for all of two minutes, and I'm ready to buy a one-way ticket out of here, so I can't say I blame him." Shane met his eyes for the first time, startled by the familiar shade of brown and green. "If you have a point, get to it. I have somewhere to be."

"Your grandmother asked me to stop by."

The bastard couldn't even come on his own accord. "Nice. So basically, you didn't want to meet me, but to save face with the wife, you dragged yourself here. Well, I wish I could say it's been a pleasure." The driver stopped at a stop sign, and Shane flung the door open.

"Wait," his grandfather held his finger up.

Shane glanced back, a million thoughts running through his head and none of them kind. He bit back all those angry words and told the man what he wanted to hear. "Don't worry. I'll tell Mimi we had a riveting conversation." He slammed the door and stormed from the SUV. He didn't stop until he was in front of Pie in the Sky.

He hoped the walk would help ease the rigid muscles in his neck, but if anything, they'd only tightened. He didn't know his father, but from what Mom had told him, he was none of the things his grandfather had said he was. Why the animosity? What the hell happened all those years ago that caused such a rift between the two?

Or was it possible good ol' Dad was everything Grandfather had said he was?

No. Shane refused to believe anything that man had said. If his dad were any of those things, there had to be a reason. Shane had a feeling it had everything to do with why Dad had left in the first place.

The sound of shoes clicked on the concrete, and Shane took a deep breath before turning toward Olivia. She was a vision in tight jeans that molded perfectly to every curve and stopped just at her ankle. Tan shoes gave her an extra four inches or so, and the navy tank she wore, though loose fitting, dipped low enough to reveal the two perfect mounds of flesh beneath.

She was a bright spot in this rather shitty day. He pushed everything else out of his mind and focused on the woman in front of him. If he'd learned anything in life, it was to enjoy the little moments before they were over.

"Sorry, I'm running late," she said. "I forgot that my only means of transportation is a golf cart. While it's much cleaner than the subways, it's not nearly as fast."

He didn't even notice. "I just got here myself," he admitted.

She tilted her head, gaze taking him in. "Uh oh. What's the matter?"

He nearly stumbled back at her razor-sharp observation. Clearly his poker face had nothing on her.

"Want to talk about it?"

"I'm not going to dump my problems on you." Olivia was his chance at fun, and unloading the shitstorm he just weathered wasn't exactly his idea of fun. It sounded more like a revisit to the mouth of the hell gates.

"Why not? I dumped mine on you yesterday and, if we're counting, the night on the train, too. I think you've earned it. Besides, there's something about talking through your problems over pie that is comforting."

Despite his strong resolve and ability to suppress his emotions, he supposed he could use a little comfort right now.

"Come on." Olivia turned the knob, rested her hand against the wood, and held the door open. "Step into my office."

Shane didn't hesitate and moved toward the door. The delicious aromas of vanilla and cinnamon surrounded him, making his stomach growl in anticipation.

The place was tiny, yet it felt as if he had walked into

someone's home. The mint green and white colors that covered the floor tiles, walls, and counter were warm and inviting.

"Hi, Miss Karen." Olivia waved as she clicked her way across the tiles.

Miss Karen's face lit up beneath her dark brown curls that were pushed back in a bandana. "Hi there, Olivia. You're spoiling me with your presence. Two times in one visit." Miss Karen rested a hand against her chest.

"I couldn't be in town and not stop in for some of your amazing pies."

In town? Did that mean Olivia planned on going back to the city? He could ask, but to ask was to care, and it was none of his business whether she was staying or not.

"What can I get you started with?" Miss Karen asked.

"Shane would love a slice of your coconut cream. He has never experienced your genius."

"Then sweetie, you are in for a treat. This is my mother's recipe and has been winning me awards before I opened these doors." Miss Karen cut a slice and placed it on a white doily that sat upon a jadeite plate. "Here we go." She handed him the plate then a fork. "Get ready to fall in love."

He had no idea why he looked at Olivia instead of the pie, but his eyes locked with hers, and the world around him dimmed.

The world came back into focus, and he snapped his gaze away from the brown depths of Olivia's eyes and concentrated on the solitary slice of pie. He had no idea what the hell that was, but he wasn't about to explore it.

"And what can I get you, Olivia? Or would you like an extra fork to share?"

"Oh no," Shane said, breaking his attention away from the brown depths of Olivia's gaze. "There is no way I'm sharing."

"Selfish!" Olivia said with mock shock that had him stifling a laugh.

"You're the one who said this pie is amazing. If that's the case one slice probably won't cut it. Go ahead. Get whatever you want. On me." Her eyebrow lifted, but before she could say anything, he reached into his pocket and handed over his debit card to Miss Karen. "Whatever you want," he repeated and gave her a wink.

Olivia ordered the old-fashioned chocolate cream pie, and they sat at one of the four tables pushed against the wall.

"You ready?" Her eyes took him in, and he liked the excitement dancing in her irises. To think she was this excited over him trying a little piece of pie. He couldn't help but wonder what kind of look she'd have in her eyes if he were to peel that low clinging shirt from her body, lick a line down to her navel, and suck on the sensitive spot where skin met panties.

The thought had him shifting in his seat. He brought his attention back to the pie and picked up the fork. "I'm ready."

"Well, go on." Olivia waved her hand at him impatiently.

He took a forkful, and when his mouth closed over the creamy bite, he was transported back to his tenth birthday and all the years that followed. Nostalgia washed over him, basking him in happy memories before a rush of sadness sucker-punched him in the chest. All he had left of Mom were random waves of recollections that hit him at the strangest of moments—eating pie, hearing a cardinal, a TV commercial. Some recalling significant times together and others just a reminder of an insignificant conversation.

It hurt to think that he'd never be able to make any new memories with her. He shoved the sadness down, refusing to allow himself to drown in the darkness for more than a moment.

He glanced at Olivia who was practically out of her seat on his side of the table.

"So?" she asked.

All he had to do was lift up slightly to press his lips to hers, use her to completely cover up the ache in his heart while he did the same for her. He controlled his carnal urge and pointed the fork at the slice. "Amazing."

Olivia shimmied in her chair, and his attention drifted to the two mounds bouncing beneath her top.

"I told you!" she announced pride lighting her face before she spun in her chair and gave two thumbs up to Miss Karen. "He loves it!"

"I knew he would. My mama's recipe never disappoints."

She turned back to him, a satisfied smile curving wide.

"You're really proud of yourself right now, aren't you?"

"Not that I ever doubted Miss Karen's genius, but I was afraid your palette wouldn't be up to par."

"I see how it is. You don't think I know a good pie when I taste one because I'm not some rich city boy?"

"That's not what I meant. All I'm saying is some people think boxed stuff is better than homemade. I didn't know what side of the spectrum you swung on." She forked a piece of her own pie, and her pink lips closed around the chocolate piece. A moan sounded in her throat just before her tongue slipped out and swiped across her mouth. *Damn.* He didn't realize how sexy eating could be. "Sorry. I always have to savor that first bite."

"Only the first bite?" If he had a taste of her, he would be sure to savor every last drop.

"The first bite is always the best."

He took another bite, enjoying it just as much as the first. "Why is that?"

"It's all the anticipation winding up into that one moment, and if it exceeds your expectations, then every bite after will, too."

"And if it doesn't?"

"Ruined."

Amusement shot through him at her bluntness. "Just like that?"

"Just like that. Now tell me…" She scooped another piece, her tongue dabbing her bottom lip again. "Why coconut cream?"

He fought the pain and sorrow of the memory and zeroed in on the happy parts. "On my tenth birthday, my mom had been working two jobs, and even though she was exhausted, she wanted me to get me a cake and sing happy birthday. Except the bakery she went to didn't have any cakes. They had bread, cookies, and pie. She said give me a pie then. But they only sold them by the slice."

"Of course."

"Somehow she managed to get the whole pie. After that, coconut cream became a tradition on my birthday. We'd go to the same bakery and get a slice every year."

A tender look crossed Olivia's soft features. "That's really sweet."

"What does your mom think of you coming here?"

He swallowed at the uncomfortable lump, pushing its way up his throat. "She passed away a few months ago."

The roundness in Olivia's cheeks deflated slightly. "I'm sorry."

"Thanks." The stubborn lump resurfaced and he ran a hand over his face to conceal the battle of emotions he was fighting.

It'd been a few months since Mom had died, and he hadn't talked about it. He couldn't afford a proper funeral, and they didn't know many people to begin with, so he had a private service for her with a few of her coworkers. That was the last time he spoke openly about her. But talking with Olivia now and sharing the good memories, it felt right. He didn't want to just share the good, though; he wanted to share with her the sad parts of his life, too, and that scared him.

"I went to the bakery after she died." He was quiet for a moment, remembering that sunny day. He'd been so mad the sun was out, but he knew it was Mom shining her light down on him. "The owner remembered me. Asked about my mom, and she told me that my mom didn't have enough money for a whole pie that first year. But she'd seen how determined my mom was to get that pie, so she told her that since it was close to closing, all pies were half off. She said she wanted to offer it at no charge, but she didn't think my mom would accept."

"Would she have?"

"Not a chance in hell." A laugh bubbled out of him, and it was a welcoming reaction compared to the ugly dry lump in his throat. It was nice having someone to talk to. He'd gone so long being alone, he'd almost forgotten what it was like to share the small joys of life with someone.

He finished off his slice and nodded to Olivia who was taking smaller and smaller bites. "What about you?"

She put her fork down and crossed her hands on the table. "What do you want to know?"

He had so many questions. Did she have a favorite spot to be kissed? Did she prefer to be in control or be controlled? Figuring it was too early into their first date to ask—not to mention it wasn't even ten a.m. on Tuesday—he went with a more basic question. "Tell me about your parents."

"You saw my dad the other night."

It was dark, and he'd only seen his outline, but the fuzzy contraptions on his feet were not to be missed. "He has great taste in slippers."

Olivia fell back in her chair. "My two-year-old niece got those for him as a Christmas gift. I can't believe he actually wears them, especially since I bought him shearling lined suede slippers that cost five times what those ridiculous things cost."

"The price of something shouldn't make it better."

She held her palms up like a scale and lifted her left hand higher. "Cheap synthetic material." She raised her right hand and lowered the left. "Luxurious shearling and suede."

Shane mimicked Olivia, holding up his left hand. "Or… no sentimental value." He lifted his right hand higher. "Sentimental value."

She finished off her last bite and closed her eyes for a moment. Her lips brushed against each other, and she sighed. "Last piece was just as good as the first." Her long lashes fluttered open, and she rested her fork back on the table. "What was I talking about?"

"Your dad's slippers."

"Oh right. I forgot on purpose." She winked, and though it was meant to be humorous, Shane found it enticingly erotic.

He cleared his throat, ignoring the pressure building beneath his shorts. "What does your dad do when he's not standing on his doorstep in monster slippers?"

"He's a history teacher at the middle school. My mom is also a teacher. Kindergarten."

"Both parents are teachers. I'm surprised you're not a teacher." She was friendly with all the townspeople, and he was sure that charismatic charm would carry over to children.

"Oh, that's not for me. I don't have the patience.

Besides, I had my eyes on city life, living the corporate dream."

"How'd that turn out for you?" he asked.

She tilted her head, a blank expression on her face. "How do you think?"

"I think it worked out for the best."

Her elbow perched on the table, and she rested her chin on her upturned hand. "Really? And why is that?"

He motioned toward her. "You have the whole city girl look down, but you're a small-town girl at heart."

Her perfectly sculpted eyebrow arched. "Is that so?"

He nodded.

"Care to elaborate? Or you going to let me wonder how you came to this conclusion about me?"

"It's simple really. I watched you yesterday with the book club. You moved right into the conversation, and it was obvious you were in your element."

"I do love the warmth of the town… how everyone always has a kind word to offer. I lived in the city for three years, and I couldn't tell you the name of one person who lived in my building. They all pretty much looked the other way when you passed them." She waved her hand. "Not that it matters now."

"At least you didn't have to say goodbye to anyone." It was why he avoided relationships. Saying goodbye never got easy. If anything, each goodbye weighed heavier on his shoulders. He'd lost so much in his twenty-six years, and he thought he'd become numb to the pain, but losing Mom nearly broke him. It was the only reason he came to

Morgan's Bay in the first place. He was searching for some sort of light at the end of the dark tunnel of his life. He foolishly thought it would be his family that brought that light back into his life. He never expected it to be the beautiful woman sitting across from him.

chapter 9

Waving goodbye to Miss Karen, Shane held the door for Olivia, proving once again to be a gentleman. She flashed him a smile as she passed and let her eyes linger on him. When she'd asked him out for pie, she hadn't had high expectations. She'd pretty much lost her faith in men, but Shane gave her hope again.

She enjoyed getting to know him. He was a gentle soul who harbored pain deep in his heart. She could see it in his greenish-brown eyes when he spoke about his mother. She sensed there was more to the story, but she didn't want to pry. At least not yet.

Shane looked at his phone. "Almost time for your first day," he said, glancing toward the pub. Connor had hired her on the spot. Barely even interviewed her. Then again, he had known her a good portion of her life. Unlike the other McConnells, Connor had gone to public school with the rest of the town folk.

"Want to walk with me?" she asked.

"We still have time," Shane said. "Besides, you owe me a kiss."

Heat rushed to her core at the thought of Shane's mouth on hers, their tongues sliding against each other. Anxious sparks skittered beneath her skin, and she bit back the smile trying to form, instead curving it into what she hoped was a sexy grin. "Is that so?"

He angled his head toward her, and though every muscle in her body was fighting her, she put up her hand.

"Kissing me out in the open on Main Street? Do you know what that means?"

He stepped closer, heat coming off him in delicious waves that surrounded her in a fiery blanket of desire. "What does it mean?" His voice dipped to a sultry whisper that had her desperate to throw her inhibitions to the curb.

"Next thing you know, the whole town is planning our relationship down to the wedding day and how many kids we'll have. Probably twins. A boy and a girl."

"Kids?"

Olivia snickered at the squeak in his voice. "Don't worry. You won't impregnate me by kissing me."

"But the town will think you're carrying twins."

"You're learning." She tapped his chest, and an electric current jolted through her veins. Shane wrapped his hand around her wrist and yanked her into the alley between Pie in the Sky and The Book Nook. He backed her into the wall, strong male consuming her. His arms caged her in, and she arched toward him, desperate for his touch.

In one fell swoop, he captured her lips, lava exploded in her chest and dispersed in heated waves. His mouth moved against hers with a carnal lust so passionate and demanding, she lost sight of everything else. All she could focus on was the hard press of Shane's lips and the hard bulge in his pants meeting the apex of her thighs.

A moan escaped her throat as his hands cupped her face and tilted her head. His tongue swiped lovingly at the crease between her lips, and she parted, welcoming the slick feel. It was a sensual dance of tongue and teeth, licking and nipping, giving and taking. He tasted of sweet coconut and confidence, kissing her with a potency she would never forget.

The way he kissed her, ravenous and precise, it was as if he'd been doing it for years. She melted into his lips, letting him take control, and not because she felt he needed to dominate, but because she wanted him to.

His body pressed into her, her back melding to the cool brick wall. It was fire and ice, heaven and hell, and she didn't want it to end. She grabbed his t-shirt, holding him close, absorbing every sensation flooding her body.

He kissed a trail from the corner of her mouth down her neck and back. The stubble on his face left tracks of passion. She didn't care. Tonight, when she was in her bed, all she would be thinking about was this kiss.

A giggle broke the cloud that surrounded them. "Don't mind me. Continue just as you were." Olivia didn't need to turn to know whose voice that was—Jean Kelly, owner of The Book Nook.

Olivia dropped her head to Shane's shoulder, embarrassed heat prickling her neck and cheeks. Shane held her, and Olivia felt his arm raise in a wave.

"Have a good day, you love birds," Jean said, and Olivia covered her face with her hands.

"Is she gone?" Olivia asked a few seconds later.

"She's gone." Shane's warm breath caressed her ear. "So… what do you want to name our twins?"

***

The first day at the new job wasn't as easy as Olivia expected She silently cursed herself for wearing heels. If she knew she'd be running back and forth to the kitchen in a never-ending rotation, she would have worn running sneakers. She'd had more of a workout running food and drinks than she ever had on her trips to the gym with her trainer.

Taco Tuesday was McConnell's Pub's most busy day of the week, and Olivia understood why Connor barely even asked her any questions before offering her the job. She dropped off a round of margaritas, wiped down a table, picked up a check, and brought it over to Shane.

He took the credit card from her, his hand lingering on hers for a moment before he pulled away. "How's it going?" he asked as swiped the card through the machine.

She looked down at her feet. "Sneakers from here on out."

"Do you own sneakers?"

She grabbed her chest in mock offense. "Yes, I own sneakers."

He held his hands up, and amusement tugged at the corner of his mouth. Her eyes hung on the movement for a moment, remembering the things that mouth was capable of. Liquid heat moved through her veins at the memory of her body up against the wall as he pressed into her.

"I've only seen you in heels." Shane's eyebrow cocked and she shook the steamy memories from her mind, refocusing on the present.

"What's wrong with my heels?"

"Nothing. I think they're sexy as hell." He tore the receipt from the credit card machine and handed it to her.

Her lip quirked at the compliment, and she resisted the urge to lean across the bar and kiss him. She held the receipt up and spun on her heel, giving a little extra sway in her step. She looked over her shoulder, catching Shane's eyes on her.

Her phone buzzed for the millionth time, and she sighed. Daniel had been blowing her phone up since the second half of her shift. It amazed her. While they were together, he didn't have enough time to check in with her, yet now that he wanted something, he had all the time in the world.

She silenced her phone, shoved it into the pocket of her apron, and moved on to her next table. As she took the order, the sound of the door opening drew her attention. She closed her eyes and sighed when she spotted her parents strolling in, perplexed looks on their faces as they scanned the pub.

Dad spotted her first. "There she is!" he announced loud enough that everyone in the crowded pub turned and looked at her.

"Isn't that your dad?" the snarky teenager whose order she was taking asked, even though he knew damn well it was.

"Aren't you too old to have Mommy and Daddy checking in on you?" The question followed with muffled laughter as his friends joined him.

Olivia didn't even bat an eye. Instead, she tapped her order pad with her pen. "Watch it Benny. Or I'll tell your dad you were the one who stole Mrs. Harrison's yard gnome."

Benny's eyes widened. "You wouldn't."

"Try me." His head fell, smirk wiped clean off his face. Checkmate.

She turned from the table just as her parents approached. Mom's dark brown eyes glistened beneath her thick bangs. "How's your first day?" Mom asked, an unspoken apology in her gaze.

"We thought we'd come and surprise you," Dad said. "Have dinner."

"I told him we should stay away and leave you be, but he insisted." Now Olivia understood the apologetic look. Dad was nosy, couldn't help himself, and she was sure her parents argued about it until Dad grabbed the keys and insisted they go.

"It's all right. We're a bit crowded tonight, though."

"It's always crowded on Taco Tuesday," Dad declared. "We can wait. If it means we'll get the best waitress." His tone rose with each word until his voice echoed above all the other chatter.

Embarrassed heat crept up Olivia's neck, and she caught Shane watching the Rick Green show. Shane's gaze met hers, and he gave her wink that she felt in her core. Not wanting to be turned on in front of her parents, Olivia broke the stare.

"Dad, you do realize we know every single person in here, right?" She appreciated his efforts, but it wasn't like there was a single person in there who didn't know he was her father.

"I'm working the room for you. Getting you the big tips."

Oh, heaven help her. It was time to corral them to a table before Dad made another declaration.

"I have a table over here." Olivia held her hand up and waved her parents forward. Once they were seated, Olivia pointed to Mom first. "Cabernet for you. and Dad, a light beer."

"Best waitress ever!" Dad announced.

Olivia covered her face with her hand. "Dad, please."

"I don't know why you let him embarrass you," Mom said. "Just do what I do and ignore him."

"Excuse me." Dad motioned to himself in a dramatic display. "I'm sitting right here."

"I'm going to go get your drinks." Olivia hurried to the bar. Shane was closing out a tab, and instead of waiting, she went behind the bar and grabbed a bottle of beer and a wine glass. She scoured the area for the wine but couldn't find it.

Shane's mouth came near her ear, an excited chill cascaded down her spine. "Can I help you with something?" A trail of goosebumps erupted as his breath caressed her skin.

"Just looking for the wine," she breathed.

He reached around her, his arm grazing the underside of her breast. His long fingers wrapped around the neck of the wine bottle, and he brought it to her.

She took it from his hold and spun around, not realizing how close he actually was. She pressed against the bar, but they were still practically chest to chest. "Thank you." She tried not to fixate on the sexy curve of his mouth, but all she could think about was their kiss. Those lips brought her so much pleasure, she could only imagine the places they could bring her if they had more time and more privacy.

As if she needed a reminder that they weren't invisible, Maria approached the bar with a smile. "I heard you two were an item," she said. "Obviously it's new, so I'm not going to pry, but Shane, Olivia is a sweet girl, and any guy would be lucky to have her."

Shane's brows furrowed in what looked like disappointment. An unexpected pang hit Olivia in the gut.

"I guess you're not pregnant," he said, and the pang turned to a rumble of laughter.

"Pregnant?" Confusion filled Maria's brown eyes.

"It's a joke," Olivia clarified before the whole town thought she was knocked up by Daniel based on the timeline. Olivia practically laughed at that absurd thought. It would never happen. She took her birth control like clockwork. Daniel insisted a child would derail his career.

Olivia filled the wine glass and held it up. "I need to drop these off to my parents."

"Oh, your parents are here? I didn't see them." Maria turned from the bar, scanning the dining space.

"You must've just gotten here, because you definitely would have heard my dad." Olivia pointed to the table in the corner where her parents were in deep conversation, eyes focused on each other and talking like the chaos around them didn't exist.

For all her dad's quirks, Mom loved him still. While Olivia got embarrassed by his antics, Mom embraced them. They were her favorite love story, and she only hoped that one day she'd find that sort of happiness that only came with years of love, devotion, and acceptance.

"I won't bother them now, but I'll stop by later to talk to your mom about her appointment. I've been trying to convince her to add a little color to her hair. I think if she goes a little lighter around her face, it'll brighten her complexion."

"It would be pretty for the summer, too."

"Exactly. I'll keep trying."

Maria headed back to her husband, and Olivia brought the drinks to her parents, placing them on the table. "Have you guys decided what you'd like to eat?"

"It's Taco Tuesday," Dad said.

"Let me guess… three tacos. One chicken and two steak. And Mom you'll have two tacos one chicken one pork."

Dad clapped, and Olivia inhaled deeply. "You're a natural," he said.

"I've been going to dinner with you my whole life, and you always order the same thing."

"Take the compliment, Livvy," Dad said.

"Compliment taken. I'll go put these in, and they should be out in ten."

"We're in no rush," Dad said. "We can even stick around and give you a ride home."

Ending the night squished into a golf cart with both her

parents was the last thing she wanted. She'd been waiting all day to have Shane alone again, so they could have a repeat of their earlier kiss. Her parents would put a definite monkey wrench in that plan if they decided to stick around.

"I'll grab a ride from someone."

"What time will you be home?" Dad asked.

It depended on how long she'd be attached to Shane's lips, assuming he'd want a second round. "I'm not sure."

"Closing time is ten, so once you square everything away, you shouldn't be home later than eleven."

"I might want to stick around with some of the crew and have a drink."

"So, midnight then?"

"I don't know. Maybe."

"I don't want to leave the door unlocked if I go to bed."

"Then don't. I have a key."

"John Andre will get upset and think someone is breaking in if the lights are out."

Olivia let out a loud sigh. "Dad, I will be home when I get there. I will be quiet, so I don't wake you, Mom, or John Andre."

"Rick." Mom rested her hand on Dad's and leveled him with a look. She didn't say anything, but the look was enough to derail Dad from the conversation.

"Just make sure to lock the door and shut the outside light off."

"That I can do," Olivia said and cut a quick glance at her mom with a grateful expression on her face.

Olivia loved her father more than anything, but the man could drive her batty. She was twenty-five years old, but he still felt the need to treat her like she was a kid.

"I'm going to go put your order in." She hurried away from the table, checked on her other customers, and headed to the bar for a quick chat with Shane while she waited on table five's drink order.

"You look stressed," Shane said.

"My parents can drive me a little crazy."

"Parents are good at that. But take it from someone who knows, one day you'll miss it."

Pain flashed in his green-brown eyes, and her heart broke for him. She couldn't imagine what it was like to lose a parent, let alone two. At times her parents made her question her own sanity, but she'd be lost without them.

"I know I would," she said. "But when you're in the midst of it, it's hard to let yourself remember that."

He placed the drinks for table five on her tray. "Trust me, I know. My mom was a royal pain in my ass." He laughed, and it was beautifully pure. "She was always on my case about something. Now I know it was out of love, but damn if it wasn't annoying as hell."

Olivia nodded. "What's love without a side of annoyance?"

"That's greeting card material right there."

"At least I know if waitressing doesn't work out, I'll have something to fall back on." She flashed him a flirtatious smile, grabbed her tray, and headed to table five. She dropped off the drinks, delivered her parents' food, and took a few new orders.

The night was flying by, and her feet were killing her. She couldn't wait to get home and collapse in bed. She still had a few hours left. She brought her parents their receipt, and Dad didn't even look at the bill, handing his credit card right over.

She went to grab it when he pulled it just out of reach. "Maria tells us you have a new boyfriend."

This town really didn't waste any time. At least they didn't have her pregnant and alone. "I don't have a new boyfriend. Daniel and I just broke up. I'm not looking for anything serious right now."

"If you give the milk away for free, no one is going to want to buy the cow," Mom said, and Olivia all but dropped to the floor and hid under the table.

"Wow, Mom. Okay."

"All I'm saying is there's nothing wrong with making a guy work for your attention. It worked for me." Mom's gaze swept to Dad's, and she smiled lovingly at her husband of thirty years.

Just as Olivia was about to run from this conversation, Shane appeared beside her. She looked at him with wide, questioning eyes.

"Did you need me to run that?" he asked, nodding toward the credit card in Dad's hand. "Sure." She plucked the card from Dad and handed it to Shane.

"Hi," Shane said to her parents. "Olivia has told me so much about you."

"She hasn't told us anything about you," Mom said

while Dad stared at Shane, his face paler than usual.

Olivia snapped out of her daze. "Mom, Dad, this is Shane McConnell."

"Shane McConnell Sanchez actually." Olivia glanced at him, and he shrugged. "My mom's last name."

"I'm sorry," Dad said. "Did you say your name was Shane McConnell?"

"I did, sir."

Dad's mouth opened then snapped shut, and Mom's eyes widened, and her face paled. . Dad shot up from the table. "I'm sorry. If you'll excuse me." Without another word, he hurried toward the front of the pub and shoved out the door.

Olivia turned to the table. Mom stood, hitching her bag on her arm. "Olivia can you sign your Dad's name and bring the card home with you tonight? Give yourself a good tip." Mom went to scurry away when Olivia jumped in front of her.

"Mom, what is going on?" Olivia looked at Shane over Mom's shoulder, looking as confused as she felt.

"I'm sure your father is just in shock."

"Shock about what?" A light bulb clicked to life in Olivia's mind. "Did Dad know Shane's dad?"

Mom glanced at Shane then locked eyes with her. "He was his best friend."

chapter 10

Words and thoughts fled Shane. All he could do was watch as Olivia's mom hurried after her husband. He tried to process the last two minutes.

Best friends.

Olivia's dad was best friends with his dad. His dad had a best friend. Why didn't Mom ever mention him? Surely she knew about the man. Shane thought coming to Morgan's Bay would provide answers, but all he was finding were more questions. To make it worse, it seemed Mom could have answered a few if she would have been honest with him from the beginning. Why did she keep everything from him? And why suddenly the change of heart when she was dying?

He looked up, as if Mom was there watching down on him and able to provide the answers, but all that was above him was the embossed tin ceiling.

Olivia's gentle touch landed on his bicep, knocking him out of his daze. He looked to her, shock in her big brown eyes and a tenderness that went straight to his heart. He swallowed at the unexpected emotion. He'd been avoiding relationships for so long, he forgot what it was like to have someone care about him.

Which was something he'd have to straighten out when his head was clear. Caring about him would put Olivia on a one-way street to regret.

"Are you okay?" she asked, her voice a mere whisper, yet he managed to hear it above the constant chatter surrounding them.

He nodded, unsure if he could form words just yet. Her hand tightened on his arm, giving a comforting squeeze. He glanced at her, curiosity overtaking his thoughts. "Did you know?"

"I had no idea. I would have said something. Thinking back, it all makes sense now."

"Why is that?"

Olivia looked around and shook her head, before guiding him toward the bathrooms and away from curious ears. The alcove for the bathrooms was small and made even smaller with the two of them facing each other.

Earlier he had thoughts of dragging her back here, lifting her up by her ass, her legs wrapping around him as he devoured her with another kiss. He finally got her back here, but circumstances were much different, though, he wouldn't mind forgetting about what he just learned and taking her mouth with his.

Desire won out, and he leaned forward and brushed his lips against hers. She squeaked in surprise, then her body relaxed, stepping into him. He ran his hand down the curve of her leg and stopped himself from grabbing a handful and lifting her against the wall. He pulled back, resting his head on her forehead, remembering why they were here in the first place.

"You were saying," he said with a smile, trying to keep the moment light.

She inhaled, her chest rising and falling, pushing her breasts higher. "If you remember that embarrassing car ride home from the train station, Milo said I had a bit of an obsession with the McConnells."

"Oh, I remember quite well. Makes me wonder if that's the only reason you tolerate me."

She swatted his chest then smiled. "Doesn't hurt."

His mouth dropped in feigned shock. She lifted her hand and pressed a finger to his chin, effectively closing his mouth. "I'm kidding."

"You didn't have a crush on one of my cousins, did you?" He'd only met Connor so far, but there were more of his generation. And Connor was a good-looking guy with a charming personality to boot.

"Jealous?"

He stole another kiss then shook his head. "Maybe."

The apple of her cheek lifted and rounded out with her smile. "It wasn't really like that," she said. "I was more obsessed with the image, the grandeur of their life. All the McConnells drove expensive cars. Connor's first car was a brand-new BMW. My first car was a ten-year-old Honda that leaked oil. All the McConnells were well put together, their pictures were in the society pages, and as a kid and a teenager, I dreamed of living that life. But my dad would get mad at me. It seemed ridiculous to me that he'd care about a silly fantasy, but now it makes sense. He'd been an outsider who'd had a glimpse inside, there was stuff he knew, stuff he kept from me."

He reached out, tucking a brown strand behind the delicate curve of Olivia's ear. "Looks like we both had parents who kept stuff from us."

"But why?"

"That's the million-dollar question."

Olivia's dad had to know something. "Can you talk to your dad? See if he'll meet me."

"I can try, but I've never seen him like that. He's not a man to up and leave without warning. He also loves to talk, so the fact that he dodged the chance…I don't know."

He cupped her jaw, running a thumb along the softness of her skin. "It doesn't hurt to ask, right?"

She blinked up, that tender look resurfacing as she stared at him. "I'll ask."

Relief Shane didn't know he was hoping for spread through him. He captured Olivia in a sweeping kiss, tilting her head and parting her lips with his tongue. It'd been long enough, and he needed to taste her one last time before they got back to work.

He felt her moan against his palm, fueling his desire for her. This time he backed against the wall, letting her have control. Her body melded to his, her round breasts pressed against his chest, and her hand snaked up his neck to settle in his hair.

Her grip tightened, and she held her mouth to his, swirling their tongues together in an erotic dance. Sparks ignited in his chest, glimmering at first than exploding and shooting straight to his groin.

His hand tangled in her hair, angling her head and seizing control, needing to take as much as she was willing to give. He took her face in his hold, and they moved as one until her ass hit the wall.

Right now, there was so much he didn't know, but one thing he knew without a doubt. Olivia Green was potent, and if he wasn't careful, she could find her way into his dying heart.

***

Olivia got home well after midnight. The outside light was still on, waiting for her arrival. She quietly opened the door and eased her way in, making sure to be as quiet as possible. She headed to her room when a shadow caught her peripheral, and she jumped back, grabbing her chest.

"Dad! Geez you scared me. What are you still doing up?"

"Couldn't sleep."

"You had kind of a shock earlier. I think we all did." Olivia sat down on the loveseat, angling toward the couch where Dad was propped up against a pillow.

Dad didn't look at her, his eyes stayed focused on the blank TV screen. "I had no idea he had a son."

"It seems not many people did. Shane's dad died when Shane's mom was only a couple months pregnant. They hadn't even told anyone yet."

"I wish I would've known."

"I wish you would have told me about him. Why didn't you?" There weren't any pictures or any stories Olivia could recall. It was his best friend. How did he go through the last twenty-five years without a mention of a man who was such a big part of his life at one point?

Dad let out a breath, running a hand over his bushy mustache. "It hurt to think about what could have been.

Raising our kids together, going on family vacations, and calling each other up with new milestones. First steps, first words, first day of school… I'll never know what that would've been like, and it pains me to think about it, so I closed it off. I never forgot about Shane. A part of him has always been with me, but I could only think of him as he was in the past, pretending he's permanently there instead of…"

A wall of tears filled Dad's eyes, and he blinked away. His lips parted like he still had more to say but was too scared to try.

He cleared his throat. "I miss him. It's easy to forget about him every day, but in the quiet moments, the moments when there are no distractions from my mind, surrounded by silence, he's there. Always there." His lips pressed together, and he nodded. A single tear fell down his cheek, and he discreetly swiped it away. "Always."

Olivia couldn't believe that in her twenty-five years she never knew Dad's best friend had died. He never talked about him. Never mentioned him in passing, or at least not that she could ever recall. When Shane's father died, her father had locked him away. She understood he did it for his own good, but she couldn't help but wonder if purposely suppressing the memory of his best friend didn't take a toll on him.

It was strange to think her parents had a life before her, but they did. And it was a life she knew little to nothing about. She had no idea if being in the dark about her parents' younger years was her fault or her parents', but either way, she was disappointed in herself for never asking them about their lives growing up.

"I'm sorry. Sorry for your loss and the pain it's caused, and I'm sorry for not knowing."

"You shouldn't be sorry about that. How were you to know?"

"I feel like I should have. I've just always seen you as my dad, and I never stopped to think that you were once a teenager with friends and a life."

"I still have a life," he said.

"You know what I mean."

"I do, but even if you asked, I don't know how much I would have told you. Some things are just better left in the past."

"Then you're really going to hate what I'm about to ask you."

"What's that?"

"Shane knows nothing about his dad other than what his mom told him. But she didn't know the man that you did. Shane just wants to talk with someone who knew his dad and can tell him about him. He tried talking to his grandfather but…"

"Didn't go well," Dad said matter-of-factly.

"How'd you know?"

"Mr. McConnell isn't exactly the warm and fuzzy type. Besides, he's the reason Shane ditched town."

Olivia rested her elbows on her knees and her head on her knuckles, leaning close in intrigue. "Why?"

"They had a fight. He was vague on the details, but it wasn't the first. This one was the catalyst that had him packing his bags and heading to California. He wanted to surf, but then he met someone, and he never wanted to come back to the east coast. He was happier than he'd been in a long time." Dad stopped talking and stared at the blank TV screen. "I can't believe he was going to be a dad. I can't believe he had a son I didn't know about. If I did, I would have made an effort to be a part of his life."

"It's never too late," Olivia said. "Shane wants to know about that part of his dad's life. You're one of the few people who can give him that."

"Maybe it's better he doesn't know."

Olivia picked at a string on the blanket draped over the arm of the loveseat before looking up at Dad. "If I were Shane, good or bad, I'd want to know."

Dad nodded. "I'd love to meet Shane properly. I promise not to run off on him again."

Relief spread through the tension in Olivia's shoulders. "He'll love that. I'll let him know. Do you want me to turn out the lights?"

Dad shook his head. "No leave them on. I'm not ready for bed just yet."

Olivia kissed Dad's cheek and headed to bed. When she was halfway out of the living room, Dad called after her. She spun back. "Yeah?"

"Is Shane the new guy you're seeing?"

They weren't technically official or anything, but he did kiss her senseless multiple times. "I guess he is."

Dad laughed beneath his breath. "Life works in mysterious ways."

chapter 11

Shane called Milo for a ride to Olivia's house. He could have easily walked, but he was in a rush. He really needed to get his own means of transportation.

Milo pulled up, and Shane, already on the front steps, hurried down. The passenger window lowered, and Milo nodded in Shane's direction. "You can sit in the front," he said.

Shane opened the door and jumped in, giving Milo a fist bump. "How's it going?"

"It's going," Milo said as he maneuvered a three-point turn with ease.

"What about you? Heard you and Liv were hot and heavy in the alleyway."

"Word really does travel fast around here."

"Harper heard from Jasper, our other roommate, who overheard Jean telling Miss Karen. Harper was pissed because Liv wasn't answering her phone all night. Chicks. Always have to be in on the gossip."

"Her ex wouldn't stop texting her."

Milo shot him a look, and his thick dark eyebrow rose toward his brown hair.

"What?" Shane asked.

"I'm surprised she's talking to you about her ex-boyfriend, considering you two are a thing."

"We're not a thing. We're just having fun."

"And you're okay being the rebound guy?" Milo asked.

"Doesn't bother me." Oliva was proving to be a great distraction for him, and he knew she was using him to forget about her asshole ex.

"I couldn't do it."

"Do what?"

"The no strings attached thing. Don't get me wrong, I've tried it. Several times, but I always wind up wanting more and getting my heart crushed."

Shane never allowed himself to get too deep, so he wasn't concerned about the heartache. Though when this was all over, he'd miss Olivia. He was getting used to having her around. "I like her. But let's be real. A girl doesn't fall in love with her rebound."

"And what about you?"

"What about me?"

"What if you're the one who falls in love with her?"

"That'll never happen." Shane simply wouldn't allow it. There were risks in loving him, and he wouldn't let anyone take that risk. Not even himself.

"All I'm saying is one person always gets too attached, and unfortunately for me, I'm the sucker. Got sick of nursing the heartache. You seem to have it under control, but if you break her heart, I will have to kick your ass. Just like I'll kick that rich asshole of an ex's ass if he ever shows his face in this town. I hope you understand."

Hearing Milo's passion in defending his friend made Shane realize what he was missing by keeping himself closed off. It wasn't enough to change his mind, though. "Olivia's lucky to have a friend like you."

"Comes with the territory. Harper would kick my ass if I didn't look out for the girls. Even still, Liv is like a sister to me."

Milo pulled up to the Green residence and put the car in park. "Need me to pick you up?"

Shane shook his head. "I'm going to walk." He had a feeling he'd need the fresh air when he was done speaking with Mr. Green. He didn't know exactly what to expect, but Mr. Green was the first person willing to speak to him about his dad.

"I'll be around if you change your mind."

"Thanks." Shane got out of the car and watched as Milo nailed another three-point turn and headed back in the direction they came from.

Shane didn't have time to overthink his walk to the door and whether he'd knock or ring the bell. Olivia flung the door open and floated down the stairs. Her long hair was pulled back, showing off her soft features and highlighting her big brown eyes. She was also five inches shorter, and as she approached Shane, he realized that her true height brought the top of her head only up to his shoulder.

He looked down at her in her sneakers and smiled. "You're half the woman you were when I saw you last."

She swatted his chest. "Shush you. My feet needed a break. This is the best I can do."

"I like it," he said. "You're the perfect height for this." He bent and kissed her forehead.

She blinked up, long lashes fanning around her eyes.

"Are you always this sweet?"

"Not always," he said. She smiled, but he felt the need to reassure her that he wasn't an asshole. "It's always genuine, though."

"Good to know." She took his hand, her slender fingers sliding between his. "Come on. My dad's waiting for you."

Shane tugged her gently, bringing her to a stop. She turned to him, curiosity tugging at the corner of her eyes. "What's wrong?"

Shane should've been running up the stairs, eager to get a glimpse into his father's life, but what if Dad wasn't the man Mom had made him out to be? What if he wasn't a good person who lived by the rules of his heart? What if he was an asshole like his grandfather? No. He couldn't be. Olivia's father didn't seem the type to be friends with someone like that.

Shane exhaled, trying to get his racing thoughts to hit the brakes, but they only seemed to kick up speed.

Not knowing about his father's roots had given Shane the chance to create a picture he could live with. What if Mr. Green painted a different picture? What if Mom lied, and Shane was nothing like him at all?

The only connection Shane ever had to the man who died before he was born were their personalities. If he found out he didn't take after his dad, then all he'd have left of him was a meaningless name and matching eye colors.

Olivia squeezed his hand and he found the strength to look at her. She'd arranged this meeting for him; he couldn't walk away now. It was time he got his questions answered.

"Your dad's okay with this, right? I don't want him to feel obligated to speak with me."

Her eyes met his. "He wants to."

He inhaled deeply and let it out slowly. "Lead the way, then."

Olivia continued up the front steps, and Shane followed her into the house. Inside she dropped his hand, her warmth lingering on his palm.

He took in the interior as he followed Olivia, and it was exactly how he pictured it. Olivia might have dressed in designer clothes and carried herself regally, but he knew, in the short time they'd known each other that wasn't who she really was. From the worn sofa to the years of scratches on the wood floors beneath them… This house was Olivia. The entire house could probably fit in the foyer of Bayview Estate, but it was quaint and cozy, and with the family pictures on the walls and the extra chairs around the small kitchen table, it was a place full of values and love.

"It's not Bayview Estate," Olivia said. "But it's home."

He hated the look of disappointment in her eyes. "I would have killed to live in a place like this growing up. A place to call my home. A familiar place filled with memories I'd always be able to return to."

Olivia's lips parted, but Mr. Green walked in before she could say anything. He wondered what she would have said, but he'd think about that later. Right now, it was time to find out about his dad.

Mr. Green stepped into the living room, and Olivia motioned between them. "Shane, this is my dad. Dad, this is

Shane."

Shane held his hand out, and Mr. Green took it and yanked him into a hug. Mr. Green held him tight. It was as if by joining together they were erecting a bridge to connect the gap between past and present.

Mr. Green stood back and held Shane's shoulders. "It's uncanny," he said. "You look just like him."

"That's what my mom used to say. She only had one picture of him, so I never had much to go off of. Sometimes I wondered if she said it to make me feel better."

"Not at all. You're his spitting image. I probably have some pictures packed in some boxes in the attic. I'll look for them."

"You don't have to go to the trouble…"

"It would be my pleasure. I've avoided the past for so long and I feel like it's time I finally take a stroll back and remember the good times." Mr. Green walked to the living room, and Shane went to follow, but noticed Olivia turning away.

"Liv," he said, and she spun toward him. "Will you…?" He didn't know how to ask her to be there with him, to give him the strength he needed to get through this conversation. But it was as if she understood him just fine.

She joined his side, and they walked into the living room together. "Please sit," he said to Shane. Shane took a spot on the loveseat, and Olivia sat beside him.

Her thigh pressed against his, and he relished in the comfort of her presence.

A little hairball ran into the room, planting his paws

apart in a menacing stance. The dog couldn't weigh more than six pounds. He barked with the viciousness of a teddy bear, and Olivia scooped him up. "This is John Andre." John Andre licked her cheek then focused his dark brown gaze on Shane. "He doesn't bite."

Shane reached out to pet the little guy, and John Andre dodged his hand, staring at him with reservations.

"Don't be a brat," Olivia said to the pup, placing a kiss on the top of his head.

Shane tried again, and once his hand made contact, John Andre leapt from Olivia's arms right into Shane's. John Andre jumped up over and over, tongue flapping, trying to get in as many licks as he could.

A giggle came from Olivia. "He likes you."

"He's a good judge of character," Mr. Green said.

A noise outside caught John Andres's attention, and he jumped from the couch and ran full speed for the door, a string of barks following.

Olivia got up and opened the door. "Go get em!" she said as John Andre took off into the gated yard. Olivia returned to the loveseat, her thigh going right back against his. He resisted the urge to rest his hand on her knee and brought his focus to Mr. Green.

"Can you tell me what my dad was like?" Shane asked.

Mr. Green ran a palm over his mustache, and when his hand fell away, a smile spread wide on his face. Relief spread through Shane at the pure joy that radiated off of Mr. Green.

"Your dad was a real charmer. Could talk his way out of any situation, and though he was raised with unlimited wealth, he was the most down to earth person I'd ever met."

"Where'd you meet? School?"

"Oh no. Shane's parents would never put him in public school with the rest of us town folk. We met when we were thirteen. I was walking home from school, and these kids were picking on me. Shane rode up on his bike and got the kids to leave. He rode alongside me as I walked home, and we discovered our mutual love of Dungeons and Dragons."

"My dad was a fantasy nerd?" Shane laughed.

"We weren't nerds."

"Dad," Olivia said. "Yes, you were."

"Maybe a little. Anyway, we started meeting up after school to play, and those kids never messed with me again. As we got older, our love for the game was overtaken by responsibilities and girls, but our friendship remained."

"Olivia said you didn't know why my dad finally left."

Mr. Green shifted in his seat, eyes lowering beneath his wired frames. "I may have stretched the truth a bit."

He didn't look like the kind of man who lied; there was a soft innocence about him, and when Shane glanced at Olivia and saw the confused look cross her eyes, he knew that his original assessment was right.

"Can you tell me?" Shane asked. Mr. Green was his only hope at this point. He came to Morgan's Bay wanting answers, and now that he was so close, he didn't want to leave until he had them.

Mr. Green ran his hands over his knees "I don't think it's my place."

"Please, you are the only person who is willing to speak

with me about my dad without brushing my questions off. I just want to know why he left."

For a moment, he thought Mr. Green would get up and walk out, but to Shane's relief, the man stayed put. "Shane was in his father's office when he stumbled across adoption papers. *His* adoption papers."

A million scenarios had swirled through Shane's mind about why his dad had left his family and an entire life behind. Never once did that scenario cross his mind.

"What?" Olivia gasped then slapped a hand over her mouth. "Sorry. Go on Dad."

Beneath the wired frames, Mr. Green's eyes leveled his gaze with Shane. "Your grandmother isn't your biological grandmother."

"He cheated on Mimi, didn't he? And the woman got pregnant?" It was the only thing that made sense. Shane looked like Connor, and there was no way he could have any of the McConnell traits without their blood running through his veins.

Mr. Green exhaled slowly. "Your grandfather and grandmother were married after eight months of dating. Your grandfather had an affair very early into the relationship. The woman got pregnant. From what I know, your biological grandmother gave up her parental rights, and Mimi adopted him. They kept the truth to themselves, and Mimi treated Shane as her son. Anyway, he confronted your grandfather. It didn't go well. Both said things that couldn't be taken back.

"I'm sure my grandfather told him he was a mistake

and an ungrateful brat." After their meeting, Shane knew in all the years since his father took off, those feelings still simmered.

"Something like that," Mr. Green confirmed. "He called me, telling me he was moving to California to get as far away from his family as possible. He asked me to go with him, but I had just met Celia, and I wanted to see it through."

"Good decision, Dad. Mom turned out to be a keeper," Olivia said, her loving tone helping to alleviate the tension in the room.

"I planned on taking a trip and meeting this new girl he told me about. But it never worked out. The last time we spoke, he said he had something to tell me, but I was home with Cindy, and she was a colicky baby. I could barely hear him over her crying, so he said he'd call me later. I never heard from him again." His voice quivered, and his eyes swelled with moisture. He swiped his eyes and stood, looking as if he wanted to run away from the conversation. "The next morning, he went out on his surfboard and never returned. The only solace I've ever been able to find in the whole awful tragedy is that he died doing what he loved."

Even though there was never an upside to death, Shane recognized the comfort in the way his dad left the world. "My mom said he could stay in the water from sunbreak to sunset."

"She wasn't kidding. Our games of Dungeon and Dragons had to be put on hold in the summer months because your dad was always down at the beach. He tried to teach me one summer when we were sixteen."

"Tried to teach you what? To surf?" Olivia barked out a laugh. "I would have paid money to see you try."

"Obviously, it didn't take." He took his glasses off and studied them before sliding them back in place. "Sometimes I wonder, if I was out there in California, if he would have been in the water that day…"

Shane understood regrets better than anyone, and he also understood falling down the rabbit hole of what ifs. "You can't think like that."

"Took me along time not to. Even now I have a hard time ignoring all the different scenarios. Anyway, is there anything else you want to know?"

Shane didn't even know where to begin. He had twenty-six years to think about it, and now that he had the chance, he couldn't pluck a single question from the pile. Olivia's finger brushed his, and the chaos in his mind settled down. A question pushed to the surface and Shane figured it was a good place to start. "What was his favorite kind of pie?"

chapter 12

Bright rays of sun filtered in through the drawn curtains, and Shane slipped into his sneakers. He opened the blinds, basking the room in light. It was nice out, with no overcast and a promise of sunshine for the entire day. It would be a perfect time to head down to the beach, but he had a more pressing issue he needed to take care of.

He'd finally gotten an answer, but once again that answer came with so many more questions, and there were only two people who could answer them. Unfortunately, Mimi didn't want to talk about the past unless they were discussing Shane's history, and the other person, was an insufferable ass.

Grandfather was out of the question. If Shane never had to see him again, it would still be too soon. And whether or not Mimi would answer his questions was still to be determined, but he had to at least try. Milo's car pulled up to the curb, and he honked once just as a text came through, notifying him Milo was there. Shane tugged a baseball cap on his head and shut the door behind him.

He got in the passenger side and gave Milo a fist bump. "One of these days I'll get a car," he said as Milo put the car in drive.

"No worries. I'm making burger money off of you."

Shane barked out a laugh. "I'm happy to support your

eating habits."

They drove in silence. Shane had a million thoughts running through his mind. Why did Mimi stay with his grandfather? Why didn't they tell his dad the truth? Why keep it from him? Mimi had said she'd had no idea Shane existed until he contacted her, so did that mean the rift between her and his father was never mended?

Milo came to a stop at the gates of Bayview Estate. He threw the car in park and ran a hand through his unruly hair. "Everything okay?"

Shane should have made more of an effort to strike up a conversation, but his head was stuck on a one-way track. "Lot of shit on my mind."

"If you need to blow steam off later, give me a call. I'll treat you to a burger."

"With my fare."

"Pretty much. I think of it as paying it forward from one friend to the next."

Shane didn't have friends. After experiencing the pain of loss, he decided it was better to go through life without forming relationships. He couldn't get hurt when he wasn't attached to anyone, but the people in Morgan's Bay were making it hard for him to keep thinking that way.

After everything he'd been through, having a friend didn't sound half bad. "I'll think about it. Thanks."

Shane got out of the car and marched up the long driveway to Bayview Estate. He'd given Mimi a heads up, so she knew he was coming; she just had no idea why.

He knocked on the door and waited. After a few

minutes, he knocked again.

Mimi's face appeared first, her blonde hair perfectly brushed and fluffed into place. "Shane, darling, come in. Come in!" She flung the door fully open and danced away. She had a martini glass in her hand and a smile on her face. "I'm having a cocktail," she called over her shoulder. "Join me."

Shane followed Mimi into the living room. Floor to ceiling windows gave panoramic views of the bay. Did his Dad play by the window when he was kid? What was his favorite toy? Did he appreciate the view when he was a teen? The larger than life house he got to live in?

Shane never cared about money or material things, but it would have been nice not see Mom struggle. He'd felt guilty when he'd gotten sick because he saw how much more of a burden Mom was handed.

Mimi stopped at a bar cart and held up a glass. "Cocktail?" she asked.

The grandfather clock in the far corner showed it was barely past noon. He enjoyed a beer or a cocktail every now and again, but he was also very aware of what he put into his body. "I'm good."

Mimi shrugged. "Suit yourself." She picked up a shaker and filled her glass, dropping an olive in to finish it off. She brought the drink to the couch with her and motioned for Shane to sit.

She took a sip of her martini then fished out the olive. She plopped the olive in her mouth and spoke around it. "What brings you here today?"

He had no idea how to broach the subject. Did he ease into it? Find a segue? "I know you're not my grandmother," he blurted. Mimi choked on the sip of martini she just took. She coughed and reached for a napkin. Shane grabbed the napkin and handed it to her. "At least not my biological grandmother," he added.

She recovered and sat back on the couch. Her face paled, the tight set of her forehead drooped slightly, and her blue eyes darted toward the window, staring out to the bay. She cleared her throat. "Who told you?" her voice was faint, strangled by what Shane could only decipher as hurt.

"Does it matter?"

"Of course it matters," she snapped. "It is no one's business. This damn town and their big mouths. They just can't help themselves. They love to knock me down because I live in the big house on the bay."

Shane had no idea where this train of thought was coming from, and he wasn't about to try and figure it out. He needed to stay on topic. "Nobody told me out of spite. They told me because I asked. I tried talking to you about my father, and you kept derailing the conversation. What else was I supposed to do? I just want to know where I came from. Is that too hard to understand?"

"No. No it's not."

"Then why did you want to keep this from me? Don't you think I have the right to know?"

She put her martini glass on the coffee table that looked like it belonged in a modern art museum. She angled her body to face him.

"I didn't say anything because I don't care what a DNA test says. I *am* your grandmother, just as I was your father's mother. I raised him. I woke up with him in the middle of the night for feedings. I stayed up with him when he had nightmares. I caught him sneaking into the house past curfew. I went to all of his basketball games and his debate meets. I devoted my life to him. So, I could give two shits what anyone says. He *was* my son, and I loved him with every breath in my body. When he…when he died, it broke me."

She downed the rest of her martini, and a tear slipped down her cheek. Shane held his hand out to the martini glass. It was as good as time as any to put his bartending skills to use. She blinked up, tears coating the mascara on her lashes. "Thank you."

He went through the motions of making a martini and handed Mimi the finished product, along with a tissue to wipe her eyes. "Thank you," she said again. "You're very thoughtful. Just like your father."

Sadness and longing consumed him. There were so many things he should have known but didn't. He sat down and waited for Mimi to look his way.

"Can you tell me about him?"

Mimi smiled, her entire face lighting up and revealing the true beauty she was beneath the years of plastic surgery. "I'd love to."

chapter 13

There were still a few weeks until the official start of summer, but the weather was as impatient as the beach goers. Olivia, Harper, Isla, and Milo sprawled out on a sheet they'd draped across the sand and soaked up as much of the late morning sun as they could.

This was one thing Olivia missed. Living in a concrete jungle, there weren't many opportunities to escape to the sandy shores of either the bay or the ocean, unlike at home where she was practically surrounded by both. Nothing could replace the feeling of her toes in the sand, not even an afternoon picnic in Central Park.

Milo lifted his foot onto the sheet, and Harper growled. "I swear it's impossible for you to keep sand off the sheet."

"You're at the beach. What do you expect?" Milo asked, brushing the sand off the corner of the sheet.

"I think I've died and gone to heaven," Olivia said on a sigh, placing her arms behind her head.

Isla turned to her side, facing them. The large hat she wore to protect her alabaster skin from the sun flopped forward, and she pushed it back into place. "Do you think this is what heaven is really like?"

Harper glanced at Olivia, silently asking who should take the question on. Isla's grandmother had been receiving treatment for pancreatic cancer. Unfortunately, they didn't detect it early, and she was already in the final stages.

Olivia pushed her sunglasses up on top of her head. "I think heaven is whatever you want it to be."

"Me too," Isla said, a slight lilt in her tone.

Harper leaned up, lifting the edge of the sheet and letting the sand fall off. "In my heaven, sand would stay off the sheet."

"Is this going to be all summer?" Milo asked.

"Depends on if you learn the concept of why we bring a sheet to the beach."

Milo dramatically rolled his eyes and flopped back, flinging his arm over his eyes.

Harper smirked, smoothed the sheet down and reclined on her elbows, looking over at Isla. "How's your grandma doing?"

A tear slid out from under Isla's sunglasses, and she swatted it away. She sniffed and sucked in a jagged breath.

"Uh, I'm going to go see how cold the water is." Milo, never one to handle emotions, jumped up from the sheet and jogged down to the ocean's edge, kicking up sand in his path.

"Oh Isla." Harper wrapped her arm around her, and Olivia came up on the other side, resting her head on Isla's shoulder. The three of them had been through a lot together, and one thing remained true—no matter what, no matter how much distance was between them, they were there for each other.

"You don't have to tell us," Olivia said.

"No." Isla took a deep breath. "I'm good." She shook her hands out and smacked them on her knees. "Sorry. She has her good days and her bad days. I bring her an arrangement every so often to brighten up the house and lift her spirit. Today I'm bringing her some snap dragons."

Isla's family owned the local florist, and Isla had been working there since ninth grade. She had always planned on moving away and starting a family, but after her breakup with Nolan, she never did.

"I bet she loves that," Olivia said.

"She does. Or at least I think she does."

"I'll have to stop by soon." Olivia adored Mrs. Garrick. She was the fun grandma everybody wanted to spend time with.

Isla's face brightened. "She would love that! She asks about you guys all the time."

Harper smiled and ran a hand over her ponytail. "That's so sweet. Does she still call us—"

"Charlie's Angels? Yup."

Mrs. Garrick had been calling their trio that for as long as Olivia could remember.

Olivia fondly recalled all the sleepovers at Mrs. Garrick's house. She always made brownies and let them watch PG-13 movies. In the summer, she would bring them to the beach and after to Pie in the Sky for some afternoon sweets. It was hard to imagine a woman who was once so full of life losing a little more of it every day.

"Maybe we could bring her to the beach one afternoon."

Isla smiled, but there was a sadness in the press her lips and downcast of her eyes. "I bet she'd love that. It's a date."

Olivia's phone beeped in her bag, and she sat up, adjusting her bikini top before digging for it. Daniel's name flashed on her screen, and she wanted to chuck her phone into the ocean. Instead she opened the text and startled when it wasn't the insult she expected.

Her eyes lingered on the words.

I miss you.

Her finger stalled in the air, unsure of what she should say or if she should even respond. He'd said some pretty awful things and now he missed her?

Her phone beeped again.

I don't expect you to believe me, but I do. Give me a chance to make this right. Come back to the city. You can stay at the apartment in Midtown. I'll have all your stuff sent over and set up for you.

The apartment in Midtown was nice. It was a stone throw away from Fifth Ave, and with three bedroom, two bathrooms and closest space in every room, it was the perfect place to recoup. It would also make life easier when she started sending out her resume and having to travel in for interviews.

It didn't mean she'd take him back. He cheated on her, and she would never forget that. But if he was willing to help her out a little, why wouldn't she take him up on her offer? She definitely wasn't going back to work for him, but maybe he could tap into his connections and get her past the resume and straight to the interview.

Confusion danced like drunken frat boys in her mind. On one hand, she was enjoying time with her friends, and then there was Shane...

But on the other hand, she needed to jumpstart her life again. While she enjoyed waitressing, it wasn't the career path she'd envisioned for herself.

"Who are you talking to?" Harper asked.

Olivia dropped her phone in her bag. "Just my dad asking when I'll be home." She hated lying to her friends, but she needed to make this decision on her own.

"I love your dad," Harper said. "You're lucky you got a good one." She stood up and nodded toward Milo. "I'm going to go push him in."

"Wait," Isla said, reaching for her own phone. "Let me get video."

The two of them ran down the beach toward Milo, and Olivia took her phone back out of her bag and typed a quick reply to Daniel. *Let me think about it.*

***

Shane drove alongside Olivia, rolled down the window, and whistled. She stamped her foot to a stop, flung her sunglasses on top of her head, and spun, hands on hips and fire in her eyes. When her gaze met his, the death stare cracked, and a smile formed.

"Oh, it's you," she said.

"Disappointed?"

Her sun-kissed skin complemented her brown eyes and highlighted her bright smile. "Not at all. I was worried you were a creeper who wandered into town." She glanced down the length of the car. "Nice wheels."

"My uncle let me borrow it until I figure something out." Shane was still shocked that after his conversation with

Mimi, Uncle Grady had popped in and willingly handed over the keys without Shane even prompting him to. He hadn't had time to stick around and chat, though, which Shane would have preferred over the car, but the car wasn't a bad consolation prize. The town was small, but walking took time, and Milo had other things to do other than driving Shane from point A to point B.

Olivia bent down, her top dipping forward, revealing a black bikini top. "That was nice of him."

Shane cleared his throat, bringing his eyes away from the tiny black swatches. "Where you headed? I can give you a lift."

She bit her lip and shyly batted her eyes. "I was actually heading to see you."

Warmth spread through his heart, and he ignored how happy her admission made him feel. "Is that so?"

She shrugged. "I knew you were talking to your grandmother today. I wanted to see how it went. See how you're doing."

He nodded to the passenger seat. "Get in. I'll tell you all about it."

He watched Olivia as she walked in front of the car. Sculpted, tan legs stuck out of jean shorts that melded to her ass. She was in flat sandals today, and while he loved the way her high heels elongated her curves, he preferred her like this. She looked more at ease.

She lifted the handle and pulled, but it didn't open. Realizing the door was locked, he clicked it open at the exact time she lifted the handle. A laugh rumbled up his throat as he hit the unlock button again just as she lifted.

Her hands went on her hips, and she angled her head down to the window. "Not funny."

"I'm not doing it on purpose." The laughter probably didn't help his case, though. "Don't touch anything." He motioned to the lock and held his hand up to her. She rolled her eyes, popping a hip while she waited.

He hit the unlock button, and she finally got in the car with an amused smirk on her lips. Her fruity, floral scent filled the car, quickly becoming a favorite of his. She placed her purse on her lap, crossed her legs on the seat and positioned to face him.

Her bikini tie stuck out the top of her shirt, and he took it between two fingers. "Coming from the beach?"

She nodded. "First beach day of the season with Harper, Isla, and Milo. Harper tried pushing Milo in the water, but he caught her and tossed her in instead." Amusement flashed in her eyes, and a jealous poke hit him in the gut.

He envied Olivia and her friendships—loved how she lit up every time she spoke about her friends. And more than that, he was jealous at every person who got to see Olivia in that tiny black bikini today.

He leaned over the console and pressed a kiss to her lips. It was supposed to be short and sweet, but desire took the reins, his palms cupping her face and pulling her to him. Her lips were pliant beneath his, and her hands thrust into his hair. Goosebumps erupted on his skin as her fingers trailed from head to neck.

His cock throbbed beneath his pants, and he searched deep inside himself for control. He. slowed the kiss and pulled back. "Hi." He smoothed Olivia's hair into place.

She bit her lip, her long lashes touching the apple of her cheeks. "Hi."

He kissed her forehead and got back on his side of the car, adjusting himself. "Where do you want to go?"

Her chin tilted, gaze focused on him, making him want to haul her onto his lap. "I don't know."

"I have an idea."

Olivia let out an excited squeal as he cut the wheel and made a quick three-point turn.

"Where are we going?"

"The beach," he said.

"I was just at the beach."

"I know, and I'm jealous I wasn't there."

She cast an apologetic glance in his direction. "I would've invited you, but I knew you were talking to your grandma. How'd that go?"

"Good. At least I think it was good. I blurted out that I knew she wasn't my biological grandma, and I think I hurt her feelings somehow."

"I'm sure you didn't do it maliciously."

"I didn't. She told me that my father was her son, even though she didn't give birth to him. She said despite what a DNA test says, she raised him, she stayed up with him, she went to all his games. She was his mother, and she is my grandmother. I couldn't argue with that."

"Are you happy now that it's all out in the open?"

He nodded. "I am, but I also understand why they didn't say anything. The adoption wasn't something she thought about. In her mind she was my dad's only mother."

"I'm happy it went well… or as well as it could."

Shane's eyes caught on Olivia's hands. She was fidgeting more than usual. "Everything okay with you?"

"Me?" Her voice squeaked. "Everything is fine. Why wouldn't it be?"

"You seem… I don't know… like something is on your mind."

"Daniel texted me." She let out a loud breath and slumped in her chair. "I wasn't going to tell you, or anyone for that matter, but I don't know. The minute I saw you I felt guilty."

"Why do you feel guilty?"

"He told me he missed me. Wants to talk. He said I could come to the city and stay at one of his apartments."

Anger from some deep-rooted area in his mind raged to the surface, and Shane's hands tightened on the steering wheel as he tried to figure out where the hell it was coming from. He and Olivia weren't anything serious. They were having fun, and the fact that she was having a conversation with her ex shouldn't have bothered him, but it did.

"He cheated on you." He and Olivia weren't together, but he respected her enough not to pursue anyone else while they were doing whatever it was they were doing. Her ex sounded like a grade 'A' douchebag, using his wealth to get Olivia back. She deserved better than a promise of an apartment.

Olivia shrugged. "I know, but a conversation wouldn't hurt."

"I would just tell him no."

Olivia laughed. "No one tells Daniel no. As he once told me everything has a price, and he's willing to pay whatever it is to get it."

"So, you're going to let him buy you back?"

"I'm not letting him buy me. If anything, I'm letting him right his wrong by allowing him to help me out. I don't see anything wrong with that. Besides, if you saw the apartment in Midtown, you'd be hesitant, too."

"That's where you and I are different. It doesn't matter to me the size of a home."

"It does a little, though, doesn't it? I mean if you had the choice, wouldn't you go for bigger and better?"

"If you're asking if I'd be happier, I can say with one hundred percent certainty, no. I base my happiness on moments and memories. And the great part about that"—he pointed to his head—"as long as I have my mind, they'll always be there. I'll never lose them, and they'll never fall apart or get outdated. They're mine and mine alone. Every memory you have is a one of a kind. No fancy apartment or material item could replace that."

She ran a hand over her purse with the unmistakable designer LV's sprinkled across it. "I guess I see your point, but I still love my bag."

"Do you love the bag or the memory of being able to walk into that store and pay for it with your hard-earned money?"

Her lip quirked, and he could tell she was thinking about that exact moment. "Have you always been this insightful?" she asked. "Or did you develop the skill over time?"

"I like to think I've always been this awesome."

A loud laugh bellowed out of her, and the pure joy was infectious. It was a sound he could never get sick of. And though the thought should scare the ever-loving shit out of him, it didn't.

He came to a stop in the parking lot and put the car in park. He turned to Olivia, taking her face in his hands. "I don't mind being your rebound, but if you plan on going back to Daniel don't string me along."

"I wouldn't do that, and besides, I'm here with you, aren't I?"

A relieved chuckle escaped him, and he reached for the hem of his shirt, yanking it over his head. "Time to find out what all the hype is about these east coast beaches."

He got out of the car and met Olivia by the trunk. She'd stripped her shirt off and was down to her tiny black bikini top. His cock twitched at the sight.

"What?" she asked. "I'm just following your lead."

He scooped her up, and she let out a string of giggles as he ran with her in his arms, hoping it wouldn't be the last time.

<h1 style="text-align:center">chapter 14</h1>

Cindy apologized for the tenth time while Olivia hurried toward McConnell's to meet up with Harper and Isla for an early lunch before her shift started.

"Cind, don't worry about it. We can get coffee another day. I'll let Harper and Isla know you said hi."

Being so close in age, Cindy got along really well with Olivia's friends, and Harper and Isla had become like little sisters to her over the years.

"Don't forget to tell them my babysitter cancelled on me, and I really wanted to see them."

"I will. Love you." Olivia hung up the call and headed inside, looking forward to another cheat day, so she could indulge in a big plate of fries. Her trainer was going to have her neck if she went back to the city, and he found out she had more cheat days than exercise.

Olivia spotted Harper and Isla in the corner table, and she made her way toward them, waving to a few familiar faces as she went. She slid onto the seat next to Isla and hung her bag on the back of the chair.

"Cindy's sorry she can't make it."

"We know. She texted us," Harper said.

"Then why did she…"

"Because it's Cindy," Isla said.

"Good point. So, what'd I miss?"

"Nothing." Isla put her menu down. "We got here not

that long ago."

Connor came over and took their order.

"I can clock in now if you need me," Olivia said as he wrote down Isla's order.

"We're good for now. Enjoy your lunch. I have Shane if it picks up."

Olivia glanced over to the bar where Shane was talking to Hal who sat in his usual seat at the far end of the bar.

Shane caught her looking and sent her a wink. She suppressed the smile, heat creeping up her cheeks. Connor headed to the kitchen, and Olivia focused on her friends.

"I bought a fish," she blurted and reached into her bag to get her phone to show them some pictures.

After Daniel's text, she thought back to their previous text exchanges. If she did take him up on his offer, she wanted him to know she wasn't a child, and she was capable of taking care of something.

"She's officially lost it." Isla took a sip of her lemon water before pushing the empty glass to the edge of the table. "I always knew it would happen, but I assumed it would be when you were in your sixties, and it would be a million cats."

"I don't even like cats." Olivia had always been a dog person...now a fish person. "And for your information, I have not lost it. I'm taking responsibility for something other than myself."

Olivia showed Harper and Isla pictures of her blue betta that she was now the proud mother of. "Isn't he adorable?" Olivia flipped to the next picture and the next.

"He's beautiful and majestic, right?"

"It's a fish," Harper said.

Olivia's mouth opened, and she hugged the phone to her chest. "He's my child."

Harper's brown eyebrows curved toward the straight line of her nose. "Why?"

Harper didn't need to elaborate Olivia knew exactly what she was asking. Olivia shrugged. "I don't know. I just… I thought…"

"Let me guess." Harper crossed her arms over her chest. "Daniel?"

"No. Yes. Maybe." She couldn't lie to her best friends, and there was no point in trying. "I wanted to prove that I can be responsible."

"To him?" Harper scoffed. "Screw him." Fire lit Harper's hazel eyes. "He's a childish prick who didn't have the balls to break up with you before inserting his dick into someone else. He can shove it up his ass."

Harper was as sweet as could be with a heart of pure gold, but she also had a more colorful vocabulary than a men's locker room.

"He told me he missed me."

Harper rolled her eyes. "Liv, you're smarter than that."

Isla tossed her blonde hair over her shoulder. "I don't know, he can be persuasive with his money and his big fancy promises."

"That's the thing…" Olivia said. "He wants me to move back to the city and stay in the Midtown apartment."

"Why?" Harper asked.

"So we can talk work things out."

"What is there to talk about? He cheated on you. End of story." Harper had always been fiercely protective of her friends, so her perturbed tone didn't bother Olivia.

"I'm not going to get back together with him, but being in the city would be good for me. I can't stay here forever."

"Why not?" Isla asked. "I am."

Olivia closed her eyes for a second. The last thing she wanted was to offend either of her best friends. "I can't waitress the rest of my life and I hate commuting. There's nothing here for me."

For some reason, Olivia glanced over her shoulder to Shane. He caught her looking and winked, sending a fiery heat spiraling to her core.

Isla turned in her seat toward the bar then spun back with a smile. "Nothing here for you, huh?"

Harper followed Isla's gaze and turned back to Olivia, a small smirk breaking at the edge of her mouth. Before Harper could say anything, Connor dropped off their food.

"Can I get you ladies anything else?" he asked.

Isla picked up a fry. "Nope, we're good."

"So what's going on with you and Shane?" Harper asked when Connor was out of ear shot.

"There's not much to talk about." Her mind flashed to their day on the beach yesterday. The feel of his bare chest against her as he carried her out to the beach, the hard cut of his abs and the way he laughed so easily as they chased each other toward the water, and how she felt when his arms wrapped around her and his lips crashed to hers...

Isla pointed at her heated face. "You're so full of it. You're getting hot and heavy just thinking about him."

"Did you sleep with him already?" Harper exclaimed.

"Shh." Olivia narrowed her gaze on her loud friends. "And no, I didn't sleep with him." The thought of Shane naked in front of her created an inferno beneath her skin. She took a sip of her water and savored the cool liquid as it flowed down her throat. "Though, I wouldn't be opposed to it."

"I hate you," Harper said. "Daniel might be an ass, and I don't trust that he's not playing an angle, but here you are with two guys vying for your attention."

"Still no luck in the online dating pool?" Olivia asked, knowing Harper's contempt was just frustration with her never-ending search for Mr. Right.

"I think I have swiped left on every guy in Suffolk County, and pretty soon I'll make my way through Nassau. I start tomorrow."

"You're going to drive all the way to Nassau? I don't care how good the sex was; I wouldn't drive that far," Isla said.

Harper rolled her eyes. "This coming from the girl who wouldn't even walk next door to get some."

Isla put her hand on the table, cut up by thorns from working at her family's florist shop. "Mr. O'Brien is adorable and all, but he's also forty-five years my senior, so no I wouldn't."

Harper tossed a fry at Isla's face. "You know what I meant."

Isla picked up the fry and ate it, a smug look settling on her pink glossed lips. "Thanks."

Shane sauntered toward the table with a pitcher of water in hand.

"Then there's Olivia who doesn't even have to travel. The sex comes to her."

Olivia kicked Harper under the table, and Harper let out a loud "Ow" as Shane approached.

"Everything okay?" he asked.

"Fine." Olivia offered a ridiculously fake smile. He eyed her curiously, and she should have known he wouldn't be able to put one over on him. "Harper was just telling us about her date tomorrow. Isn't that right, Harp?"

Harper narrowed her eyes at Olivia, but Olivia shrugged it off.

"Anyone need a refill?" Shane asked, having no idea what he just walked into.

"My shift is almost starting." Olivia stood from the seat and gathered the dishes. There was no point in sending in the bus boy when she could handle it.

Shane tossed a rag over his shoulder and placed the pitcher on the table before taking the tray from her hands. "I got it."

"*Right* to her," Harper said on a sigh.

Confusion tugged at Shane's brow, but he didn't question it.

"You have to excuse Harper. She's known to have random outbursts," Olivia joked, and she knew if she was still sitting Harper would have given her a swift kick to the shin.

"Everyone has their thing," he said. "Well ladies, it's been a pleasure. Maybe next time I can join you."

"That'd be great," Harper said. "We can drill you about your intentions with our friend.

Olivia, wishing she was at the table to give Harper another kick, turned to Shane instead. But he didn't skip a beat. An amused smirk spread across his face. "I wouldn't expect anything less." He tipped his head to them. "You ladies have a wonderful rest of your day."

His hand rested on her waist as he went to move around her. He leaned down, his warm breath drifted over her neck, and the intoxicating smell of sex and man surrounded her.

"Excuse me," he said.

Trying to spark the transmitters that went from her brain to the rest of her body, she stood frozen for a moment, taking in the closeness and absorbing the heat that poured off of him. Finally, she remembered how to move and she stepped aside; his hand lingered on her waist for a second more.

His gaze slammed into her. The smile on his lips was so devastatingly handsome that she had to swallow down the urge to drag him out of sight so she could lick the upward curve of his mouth.

Harper cleared her throat, and Olivia jumped back from the intensity of Shane's gaze, knocking her ass right into the table. The legs screeched, the table jerked, and glasses swayed. Harper and Isla both reached for the wobbly glasses, preventing a disaster.

Heat clawed up Olivia's neck, and Shane just smiled before walking away.

Olivia turned to her friends. "I'm sorry."

"Don't be," Harper said. "I'd be a walking wet noodle if a guy looked at me like that."

Olivia fell into her chair.

"What's the matter?" Isla asked.

"I shouldn't be falling for another guy when I still have an unfinished mess with Daniel."

Harper shook her head. "You wasted three years of your life on that asshole. I think you owe it to yourself to see it through with Shane."

"I have to agree with, Harp on this one," Isla said.

"That's a first," Harper joked.

"But what if Shane is my rebound?" Olivia asked, though the thought actually hurt her heart. She really liked Shane, and she didn't want him to be that guy, and not just for herself, but for him, too. She didn't want to string him along.

Harper blinked up at her. "What if he's not?"

chapter 15

Early afternoon quickly slid into evening as Olivia hustled from one table to the next, taking orders and dropping off drinks and food. One of the waitresses called off, leaving Olivia with a full house to manage alone. She didn't mind. She loved constantly being on the go, chatting with people she's known her whole life, and making money while doing it.

The heated exchange between Shane had lingered with her all day. Every time she glanced in his direction, her temperature went up a few degrees, and when he was near, her body was an all-out inferno.

The door opened, and Olivia turned to greet the customer. Ice settled in her veins, jagged shards expanding and compressing her lungs.

Daniel strolled in, eyes scanning like a predator. She didn't want to be found, not yet. She hadn't made a decision on his proposition yet. He'd want an answer. She could run, but if she ran away from him now, he'd just keep coming back. There was a reason he was as rich and successful as he was.

She took a deep breath, forced her mouth into an emotionless line, and approached him.

"Daniel, what are you doing here?"

He looked her over from head to toe, his eyes lingering on her sneakers then up to her apron. His nose wrinkled like he smelled something bad. "I was in town and thought I'd stop by and see if you thought about what I had said."

She should have known his impatience would bring him to her eventually. It's not like she was in another state; she was only a car ride away. Though, even if she was in another state, she doubted that would deter him. He'd hire a helicopter like he did when they had dinner with a client in DC.

"Not yet. Honestly, I've been really busy with work, my parents, my fish. I got a fish."

"You don't even like fish."

"That's not true."

He met her eyes with a charming smirk. "When we went to that sea life fundraiser at the aquarium you bitched the entire time about the smell."

"Because it stunk in there, but my fish doesn't smell."

"Why don't you bring your fish with you to the Midtown apartment? I'll even upgrade its tank and get it something fitting to match its new zip code."

Olivia thought about Shane's words from the other day. "I'm not going to let you buy me back. After everything, I don't think you could afford me."

"Sweetheart…" He moved toward her, lifting her chin with his finger. "You know I'll give you whatever you want, but I'm not trying to buy you back. I just want to talk. Please."

She inhaled deeply. "Okay." Olivia showed him to a table and slid into the seat across from him. She tried to keep her gaze away from the bar, but her eyes betrayed her and wandered to the one person she didn't want to see right now.

Shane's eyes caught hers, and she could see the curiosity in the brown-green depths. Daniel's touch jolted her attention away from Shane and back on him. He took her hand, lacing their fingers together. "I miss you. The apartment has been really quiet without you there."

"That was your doing. You brought another woman into our home."

"I made a mistake. I was out celebrating, had one too many drinks, and I fucked up. My biggest regret is that you were home to see it. I never wanted to hurt you. You got to believe that."

Her heart tugged in two different directions. Daniel was familiar, and she'd given him three years of her life. But then there was Shane, and just the thought of him lit her world on fire. But what if Harper was wrong? What if Shane was her rebound, and she'd thrown away everything Daniel could give her for a chance at love, only to be left with absolutely nothing when Shane decided the fun was over?

"What about all those awful things you said?"

"I was angry at myself, and I tried to justify my actions. I was an idiot."

"Yeah, you were."

"And I'm sorry. We were great together," Daniel said, pressing a kiss to her knuckles. "And we could be great together again."

"I don't know…"

"Yes, you do. Don't be difficult." The tone in his voice

changed for a quarter of a second, but Olivia caught it.

"I'm not," she said with defiance.

"You mean to tell me you're actually debating staying in this shithole over living in a sixteen hundred square foot apartment off of Fifth Avenue?"

"Yes," she admitted.

"You're doing this out of spite."

After all that had happened, he still thought everything she did was with childish intent.

"No, Daniel, I'm not." She stood from the table, wiping her hand down her apron to smooth out the bunched material.

"Olivia, please."

"Why don't you tell me why you're really here." If he really wanted to be with her, he'd give her space, let her figure things out on her own. He was pushing this too hard. What was his angle?

Daniel sighed, letting his hands fall onto the table. "You remember my business associate, Mr. Abrams?"

"Yes." He was a lovely man who prided himself on loyalty and family. They'd had dinner with him many times. Every time he'd ask Daniel when he'd make an honest woman out of Olivia.

Realization smacked her across the face in a hard, cold hit. "You want something from him, don't you? And you want me to tag along and give the façade like you're some family man."

"We're having dinner Friday night, and he requested your presence."

"Just tell him we broke up."

"I can't do that."

"Why not?"

"Because he's old school, and if he doesn't think I can commit to a relationship, then he's not going to invest the half a million dollars I need from him."

"Relationships end. Just tell him I broke up with you."

"I am not going to do that."

"Then I don't know what to tell you. I'm not going to go to dinner with that nice man and pretend that you didn't cheat on me."

"Can you please, for two seconds, think like a reasonable adult and not a—"

"I swear to God if you say child, I'm going to knock your teeth out."

Daniel tugged at the cuff of his shirt sleeve. "That's nice, Olivia."

"I'm done being nice to you. Now if you're not going to order anything, I'm going to have to ask you to leave."

He picked up a menu.

"What are you doing?" Olivia demanded.

"I did not drive all the way out to the east end for you to dismiss me. We have things to discuss, and I'm not leaving until we do."

"You are impossible, you know that?"

"What's good here?" he asked, opening the menu. He pulled his hand away and made a face as he rubbed his fingers together, lip curled in disgust. "Do you pay extra for the grease or is that just an added bonus?"

"It's extra. I'm sure you can afford it."

"Cute." He looked at the menu, taking his damn time.

"The burgers are good," she said. The faster he ordered, the faster she could get rid of him.

"You know I don't eat that shit. It's poison to your heart."

"Funny, I thought your heart was already poisoned."

Daniel put the menu down and turned to her. He reached for her hand, and she jolted back. With a sigh he let his arm drop onto the table. "Look, I know you're upset."

A laugh erupted out of her. "Upset? You're damn right I'm upset! You cheated on me. You lied to me. You strung me along for three freaking years."

"For three years you got to live in a penthouse over the city, work at one of the fastest growing companies in the country, rub noses with some of the most elite people in the world, and I didn't hear you bitch once the entire time."

She didn't. Now looking back, she let countless things go, reminding herself how good she had it, and Daniel's missteps were due to the fact that he was under a lot of pressure. It was nothing more than excuses, so she didn't have to leave her lifestyle behind. He was right. She didn't bitch because she was convinced having money meant she wouldn't have to worry about anything else. Money fixed everything. Except when it didn't.

"I was blinded by the opulence of your life, but the fog has lifted." She swiped the menu out of his hand. "You're getting a burger. If you don't want it, you can leave."

***

Shane couldn't take his eyes away from Olivia and the guy in the suit. He didn't have to ask; he knew in his gut it was her ex. The guy looked like a total jackass. From his slicked back blond hair to his oversized Rolex encrusted in diamonds and down to the cufflinks at his wrists, he was the epitome of flaunting wealth.

Connor was loaded, yet he still got his hands dirty in the kitchen. Shane would bet every cent in his savings account that Daniel never got his hands dirty. He probably hired people to do things like that for him.

A hand clamped his shoulder, and Connor came around. "How's it going, cuz?"

"Everything's good." Shane poured a glass of wine for Jean and pushed it across to her spot at the bar.

"Then why are you staring daggers over at that table?"

Shane swore he saw Jean turn her ear to their conversation, so he moved farther down the bar, his attention still locked on Olivia. "I'm pretty sure that's her asshole ex, and from what she's told me, I don't trust the guy."

'That explains why you look like you're ready to jump over the bar and gut someone."

"I'm not an animal." Shane laughed. "I would like to smack that smug look off his face, though."

"I know his type," Connor said. "Unfortunately, they're in our family."

"More cousins?" Shane asked.

"Yup." Connor grabbed a pint glass and filled it up a quarter of the way with Hippidy Hop, an IPA from Five

Leaf Brewery, before taking a sip. "Gabe, Bryce, and Dixon are Uncle Patrick's kids. They live in Connecticut, but come summer, they'll be popping their heads in here for free beer."

"I can't wait to meet them." Shane didn't try to hide the sarcasm in his tone.

"They're not bad. Not as cool as me, but not many people are."

"How many more cousins do I have?" Shane kept his eyes on Olivia.

"Other than those three, there's Aunt Bridget's kids, Abbey and Brianne. Stick around long enough and you'll meet them all. Mimi has a big family get-together every year to kick the summer off."

Olivia stormed from the table and into the kitchen. Shane patted Connor on the chest. "Cover me for a second."

He hurried after her. She thrust her ticket at George who was manning the grill and about-faced it right into his chest. His hands gripped her biceps, and he held her back.

"Whoa," he said. Fire burned in her eyes but softened when they settled on him. "You okay?"

"Fine," she growled.

He pressed a finger to the edge of her lip. "The tightness here says otherwise." His finger trailed the perimeter, and the fire simmered out completely.

"My ex is here," she admitted.

Shane's face hardened. If the asshole did anything to upset her more, he would toss his ass out into the street. "I'm guessing you're not going to go back to the city with him?"

She scoffed. "I should have known that with him there is always strings attached."

"Want me to get rid of him?"

"How? He won't leave. I told him he couldn't stay if he didn't order anything, so he put an order in."

"Refuse service."

"I can't do that."

"I'll bring his food to him then. Stay back here."

Her gaze immediately went to the red exit sign above the back door. "We're short-handed to begin with. Besides I can't keep running from my problems."

A protective urge came over him, wanting to carry her away from here, but he knew she needed to settle things with her ex. "I'll be behind the bar if you need me."

"Thanks, but I need to do this on my own." She kissed his cheek and pushed through the kitchen doors. Pride swelled in his chest as she marched into the lion's den.

Shane fully respected Olivia's wishes to handle her ex on her own, but that didn't mean he couldn't stand in his place behind the bar and continue to observe.

Olivia's hands went up in front of her, moving as fast as her mouth. Anger tightened the skin around her eyes. Shane took a few drink orders but kept his attention on Olivia.

"Go to hell," Olivia's voice floated over the chatter of the pub. Her face twisted in rage. Her lips continued to move, but Shane couldn't hear her over the chatter. She spun on her sneaker away from the table, and Daniel grabbed her wrist, yanking her back to him.

Shane's body jolted forward, but he dug deep and stopped himself. Olivia wanted to handle this on her own, and he wouldn't take that away from her. He picked up the rag, needing to keep busy, and wiped down the empty space of bar in front of him.

"Leave me alone!" Olivia wrenched her arm away from him, and any control Shane had snapped. He catapulted himself over the bar and didn't stop until he was firmly planted between Olivia and her ex. Confusion marked Daniel's face, and the chatter in the pub came to a deafening silence.

Shane stared into the asshole's eyes, refusing to show any sign of fear. He didn't fear people who hid behind wealth and knew nothing about real life struggles. "She said to leave her alone."

"Who the hell are you?"

"Shane, and you must be Daniel, the douchebag that was dumb enough to let Olivia go, but you know that, don't you? Because why else would you be here?"

Daniel stepped toward him, but he didn't back down. He'd faced deadlier things in his life to let a custom-tailored suit intimidate him.

"None of this is your business."

"That's where you're wrong. It became my business the minute you walked in that door. And it definitely became my business the minute you grabbed her."

Daniel looked around him to Olivia. "Do me the one favor, and you can come back to my place and take anything you want."

Olivia blinked up, uncertainty in her big brown eyes. Shane's heart sunk. After everything, she was going to walk out the door with this jerk?

"I…" She shook her head, shoulders rolling back, and stood to her full height. "I don't want any of it."

Shock spread through Daniel's face. "You have got to be kidding me."

She stepped toward him, never once cowering at his vengeful gaze. "I love my job in this 'shithole', and I make a decent salary. I may not have the things you gave me, but I don't need them. I have my family and friends who love and care about me—not to mention the people of this town who support me. Everything else is meaningless."

Self-confidence looked amazing on her. She glowed with poise and conviction, and he'd never been more attracted to someone. The wall around his heart cracked, hope and love forcing their way inside. He'd worry about it later. Right now, he needed to get rid of the trash.

"You heard the lady. She doesn't want any of it, including you, so why don't you leave?"

He pulled at his shirt sleeves and adjusted his stupid cuff links. "I'm not done eating."

Shane grabbed Daniel's hand, snatched up what was left of the burger, and slapped it down into his palm. "You can take it to go." Shane shoved him toward the door, and Daniel smacked his hands away, the burger going airborne with the motion.

"I don't know who the hell you think you are, but your

ass is mine. Where's the manager?"

Connor uncrossed his arms in his spot behind the bar and gave a wave. "That would be me, and whatever my cousin says, I back him up a hundred percent."

"You shoved me. That's assault. I'll have you arrested." Daniel reached for his phone.

"You can try." Connor stepped out from behind the bar. "But from what I saw, you attacked Olivia, and Shane was defending her."

Disbelief shone in his eyes. "That is not what happened."

"Is it not?"

"That's what I saw," Jean called from the end of the bar.

"Me too," Maria said.

"Me too," the chorus around the pub echoed.

Olivia stepped in front of Shane, and he didn't stop her. This was her battle, not his. He shouldn't have gotten involved in the first place, but seeing Daniel's hand on her wrist tossed out every rational thought. .

Olivia smirked. "Wouldn't want to tarnish your good name, now would you?"

Daniel stared at her, angry daggers shooting from his eyes, but Olivia didn't back down. She stood tall, facing the man who betrayed her with the grace and strength Shane knew she had from the moment he met her.

"It's probably best you leave."

The entire pub's attention focused on them and Olivia firmed her stance. Pride erupted in his chest as Olivia refused to back down.

"It's only a matter of time before you come crawling back," Daniel spat.

"Never going to happen."

"We'll see about that." Daniel threw a twenty on the table and stormed out. The door slammed shut behind him and the entire pub erupted into applause.

"Good riddance," Jean called out.

Olivia picked up the twenty. "All that money, and he's a terrible tipper."

Shane laughed at her ability to crack a joke after the tension that filled the room only seconds ago.

Shane touched Olivia's elbow, making sure not to grab or yank her like Daniel had. "You okay?"

She took a deep breath and let it out slowly. "I think so." She looked around at the crowd. "I have to check on my tables."

"Do what you have to do. We can talk later, if you want."

"I'd like that."

She lifted on tiptoes and pressed a chaste kiss to his cheek. "Thanks," she said, and he watched as she hurried off to the kitchen, confidence in every step.

***

Olivia's hands shook at the array of emotions battling it out in her mind. Part of her was throwing a party for being able to stand up to Daniel, but the other part of her? That part was a damn mess mixed with lingering rage and embarrassment.

Shane had already seen her at her worst; nothing could beat that day on the train. Still, having him witness the disaster that was her relationship with Daniel was humiliating. It's why she ran off to the kitchen. She didn't want to face him. Especially since it didn't dawn on her until today how emotionally abusive Daniel was. He used words and material possessions to manipulate her, and she let him. It was why they lasted for three years. She never challenged him. Never told him no and always praised him and his accomplishments.

She was ashamed for how long she allowed it to go on, but she was also proud at how she finally found the strength to see beyond his manipulation and the courage to stand up for herself.

The rest of the night moved by in a blur, bouncing from one table to the next until the last customer left. Olivia shut the door behind them and collapsed in the closest chair.

Strong fingers dug into the tense muscles along her shoulders, and she closed her eyes, relishing in the relief. She didn't want to open her eyes and come back to reality. She wanted to stay in this little cloud of heaven for as long as possible. The minute she let the world back in, she'd have to talk to Shane about tonight, and she was still too embarrassed.

Warm breath stroked her ear. "Let's get out of here. I'll give you a ride home."

She wanted to go anywhere he wanted to go, but being in a car with him, there'd be nowhere to run. "I have to help—"

"Connor's got it under control." He slid his hand down her arm and laced his fingers with hers, giving her a little tug of encouragement.

"But—"

"Go!" Connor yelled from the kitchen.

Shane smirked. "Told you."

"Let me just grab my bag." She stood, slowly releasing Shane's hand as she walked backward. Maybe they didn't have to talk at all. Their fingers unlaced, and she hurried to get her belongings before meeting him at the door.

A cool ocean breeze met her as Shane opened the door and she stepped out into the night. Spring still clung to the air, and while it was a bit chilly, Olivia welcomed it over the oppressive humidity that was bound to appear soon.

Main Street was empty. All the businesses were dark, and the only light that still shone bright was over McConnell's. In a few weeks all that would change as people made their way out to the east end for their summer getaways.

Goosebumps popped up along her arms, and she hugged herself.

"You cold?" Shane asked.

"A little," she admitted.

He fell in pace behind her, his large hands rubbing up and down her arms, creating friction and warmth. "Better?" he asked.

"A little."

He wrapped his arms around her, his heat encompassing her. A fiery trail moved along her skin, sparking little fires of desire in its wake. She'd never been turned on so easily, but when it came to Shane all he had to do was touch her, and she was ready to rip her clothes off.

It was like that with Daniel in the beginning… or at least she had thought it was. The more she looked back, she realized their hot and heavy sexcapades had more to do with the thrill of would they or wouldn't they get caught. With Shane, there was no pretense.

She stopped walking and turned in his arms. His eyebrow furrowed, his lips parting, but before he could say a word, she crashed her lips to his. All her inhibitions that she'd thrown to the curb suddenly gathered and jumped back in her mind as if she used up every last ounce of courage she had today.

Daniel's judging eyes flashed behind her lids, making her dissolve into a puddle of self-doubt. What if she was being too aggressive? What if the raw passion came from Shane and his desire to be in control?

She gave up control, trying to follow Shane's lead, but his mouth stopped moving. He pulled away, cupping her face, and angling her to look at him.

"What was that about?" he asked.

"I wanted to kiss you."

"And I wanted to kiss you, too, but one minute I'm kissing you, and the next I'm kissing a soggy dishtowel."

"A soggy dishtowel?" She playfully smacked his shoulder.

"Flaccid, moist, uninterested," he teased, moving her toward the side of the building. She knew what would happen the minute her back hit that wall, and she wanted it. His finger traced the outline of her face, up and over the curve of her ear and lingered near her lobe. "Want to talk about it?" he asked.

"Talk about what? How you think I'm flaccid, which is the most unattractive word imaginable."

His lip curled upward in an amused grin. "I meant what's going on up here." He tapped her head lightly. "And flaccid *is* an ugly word. But one minute you were with me, and then suddenly you were a million miles away."

Her head dropped at his words. He was right. She let her mind take over, filling her with self-doubt and uncertainty instead of allowing herself to be in the moment.

"I know we're having fun," he said. "But I'm selfish, and I don't want to share you with Daniel either."

Taken aback her head snapped up, smacking Shane square in the nose. A loud umph came out of him, and his hand shot against his face. He moaned and mumbled a few indecipherable words, but if Olivia were to guess, they weren't getting a PG rating.

"I am so sorry." She reached for his face, wanting to take away the pain, but also wanting the wall to swallow her whole. "Do you want me to kiss it better?"

"Depends on who's kissing me. You or the soggy towel?"

She brought his nose slowly to her face and brushed a kiss gently across it before moving down to his mouth. His lips yielded to hers, letting her keep control, and this time she took it. She thrust her fingers into his hair, holding his head close and angling it to deepen the kiss.

The electricity she'd come to expect between them flickered to life as their tongues met in a slick erotic tangle. She moved into him, arching her center to his, feeling the hard press of his growing erection.

She pulled back slightly, nipping at his lip. "How was that for a soggy towel?"

"That was no damn towel. That was all you."

She smiled and blinked up, catching his brownish green eyes. "You don't have to share me with Daniel," she said. "You saw what happened tonight. We're over. We've been over for a while."

He tapped her temple. "But he's still in here."

"I don't want him to be."

"Then don't let him."

Olivia laughed. "If it were only that simple."

"It can be."

"For three years, I tried to be everything I thought he wanted. The sad thing is, I didn't even realize I was doing it. I've never felt comfortable in my own skin. I've always thought if I was just taller, thinner, had blonde hair, curly hair, if I was smarter, sexier… I guess what that all means is I don't think I'm good enough."

Shane's hands came around her waist, holding her close, but not close enough that she couldn't look deep into his eyes. "You are good enough and whenever Daniel or anyone else pops in your head and makes you think you're not, think of this moment. Right now. Think of my words. You, Olivia Green, are more than good enough. You're pretty damn special."

The sincerity in his gaze melted her heart and gave her the confidence to pin him up against the building and kiss him until they were breathless.

chapter 16

Shane slowed the car in front of Olivia's house, and she shifted in her seat. He wasn't ready to say goodbye, but at least he'd have the memory of their earlier kiss that turned into a full on make-out session until Connor cleared his throat as he walked to his own car.

Olivia bit her lip, plump and swollen from their workout. "I'm not tired." Three unassuming words that were filled with so much promise.

"Me either," he said. "I can keep driving… or we can go back to my place."

Crimson crept up her neck and filled her cheeks. Her eyelashes fanned down. "Your place sounds good."

He turned the wheel toward the road and continued on. Olivia's hand crossed the console and rested on his thigh. His cock came to attention, pressing desperately against his zipper. He took a deep breath, but when her hand inched ever so slightly toward his throbbing erection, a moan rumbled up his throat.

Desire sparked, hot and strong, making it a sheer determination of will to keep from pulling over and lifting her onto him. He wanted to explore her, savor every inch of her body, worship it the way it deserved. All of which he couldn't do from the front seat of a car.

Her fingers massaged and crawled up and down the bulge, finally closing around his length. The car drifted, and he quickly corrected the wheel, bringing his hands back to ten and two.

Olivia giggled, and *God* the things he was going to do to her. But right now, he needed to get to his place in one piece. He rested his hand on hers, peeling her off him. She protested with a moan of disappointment.

"Let me get us there safely, and then you can explore as much of me as you'd like."

"You're a safety-first kind of guy, then?"

He kissed her knuckles and flashed her a smile. "Always." *Shit.* His hands tightened on the steering wheel as realization dawned on him. "There wouldn't happen to be any gas stations open now would there?"

"Not in town. Why?" She leaned over, her fruity floral scent making his already hard dick even harder. "You have three quarters of a tank."

He groaned as he shoved his urges down. "I don't need gas."

"Then why do you need…" Understanding dawned on her face. "Oh! Condoms. Duh. No worries." She reached into her monogrammed bag and pulled out an unopened box. "I have some."

His eyebrow lifted without prompt.

"Not that I planned tonight or anything," she said. "Harper gave them to me. She had extra." Every time Harper went on a date, she made sure to be prepared. Unfortunately, most of the dates were duds, and she was just accumulating a large collection of unused, unopened condoms since she kept forgetting to keep the boxes in her car.

He snatched the condoms from her hand and slipped them into his pocket. "You guys are really close, huh?"

Olivia nodded. "Harper and Isla are like sisters to me. Except they don't snap at me as much as my own sister does, they don't borrow my clothes and get stains on them, and they don't guilt trip me nearly as much as Cindy does."

"Is Cindy older or younger?"

"Older. She's married. My brother-in-law Zane is a saint. My sister can be a bit of a pain in the ass. Then there's Jolie, my niece. We call her, Jojo. She's my little buddy."

Shane listened as Olivia spoke about her family, warmth and love flowing through her tone.

"You're lucky," he said, "to have so many people care about you."

"What about you? I know your mom passed, and obviously you never knew your dad, but any other family other than the McConnells? Friends you left behind in California?"

Shane ran a hand over his face. All his friends were dead, and it was the reason he steered clear of making new ones. Until he came to Morgan's Bay, and Olivia so effortlessly planted herself into his life.

"I have a great uncle in Portugal, but he's old, and when I call, he has a hard time remembering who I am."

"What about friends?"

If Shane told her about his friends, then he would have to tell her about his childhood and how he lived in and out of hospitals. It was a time in his life that was very much a part of him. Disregarding that part of his life would be the equivalent to cutting off one of his limbs. But that didn't mean he liked to talk about it. Given the option, he would keep that part of him to himself.

He liked the way Olivia looked at him, and he didn't want her to feel sorry for him. He didn't want her to know the pain and uncertainty that his childhood illness caused nor those same emotions that followed him into adulthood.

Luckily, the house came into view. He pulled into the driveway and killed the engine. Instead of answering Olivia, he reached across the console, snaked his hand around her head, and crashed his lips to hers. A surprise moan slipped from her throat and muffled against their lips. He thrust his tongue inside her mouth, going deep, licking and tasting, taking his fill.

Pressure built in his balls, and his cock throbbed with need. With all the things he wanted to do to her, he needed her inside, away from the prying eyes of the neighborhood. He forced himself to pull back from the sweet taste of her lips and fling his door open. He was around to the passenger side before she even had a chance to react.

He had every intention of scooping her up, but Olivia didn't give him a chance. She leapt from her seat and into his arms, driving him backward with a force that triggered the ravenous animal inside him. He gripped Olivia's ass as her legs wrapped securely around his center. He managed to swat the door shut before carrying her toward the house.

Her teeth bit into his lip, pain and pleasure battling it out. Her tongue swiped against the tender flesh before dipping into his mouth, searching and exploring. Their tongues met in hot strokes, fueling the growing inferno flaring to life inside him.

The insecurities from earlier that caused Olivia to reserve her wild nature were gone, and all that was left was this sexual being who was confident and free. This was the Olivia he knew. The Olivia he needed. He'd felt dead for so long, and she gave him life.

He followed, allowing her to guide him toward the apex of bliss. Her legs tightened around his waist, and she arched against him, rocking her hips in a needy rhythm.

Inside, the house was dark, except for the faint glow of the streetlight. He didn't bother flipping on a light; he knew his way, and nothing was going to slow him down until Olivia's back was on his bed, and he was hovering over her.

Olivia's legs unhooked, and she slid down his body. The loss was instant, but when she landed on her knees, fingers fumbling with his zipper, any coherent thoughts fled. The sound of the zipper echoed in the silence. With one hard yank, his cock sprang to attention. She licked her lips before taking him in her mouth.

His body tensed at the pure pleasure that ricocheted through his groin, spreading out and consuming his entire body. Weakness threatened his knees, but he found the strength to keep standing, keep enjoying every stroke of her mouth down his hard length.

Her tongue swirled around his tip, a crescendo of desire wracking his body. She sucked gently, her fingers trailing up his thigh and settling around his base. Her mouth and hand moved in sync, creating a storm so intense, so powerful, Shane would be obliterated if he didn't stop her.

He rested his hand under her chin, urging her to look at him. Big brown eyes blinked up, and he nearly blew it. "My turn," he growled.

She got to her feet, her eyes half-mast and heavy with lust, lips swollen. "Okay." There was a sexy lilt to her voice that captured his heart and held it hostage. He ripped his shirt off, stepped out of his pants, and grabbed the condoms. He hooked his hand around her, scooping her off her feet, and with determined strides, he had her on his bed.

A giggle popped from her lips when he placed her down, and he swore it was the sweetest sound he'd ever heard. He kissed her then, plundering and devouring and taking everything she'd give him. He wanted her body, heart, and soul which was selfish as hell since his life was so uncertain. But right now, he didn't care about the future; all he cared about was the here and now.

His finger looped into the hem of her shirt, and he pulled it over her head, discarding the fabric into a puddle on the floor. His eyes raked over her body, and he swallowed at the red silk bra that covered two small mounds of perfection. He dipped his head, dragging his tongue along the place where skin met silk.

Olivia moaned, her body arching. Small fingers dug into his shoulders as he reached behind her and unhooked her bra. He removed one cup at a time, revealing pink, pert nipples. He dipped his head, taking the tightened bud in his mouth, licking, sucking, and nipping. Sweet pain nipped at his head as her fingers delved into his hair and yanked. Her body pressed up, head fell back, and a long, sexy as sin moan echoed through the room.

Wanting to make her cry out, he slid his hand down, dipping under the waistband of her pants. He swiped his finger across her swollen, wet folds, greedy for more of her. He dipped his finger into her wetness, and her body jolted, her nails cutting deep into his shoulder.

She felt like paradise, and he needed to see her bare and ready. He yanked her pants down, and she helped kick them off. His cock pulsated at the sight of a matching G-string that hugged the curve of her hips.

"You're trying to kill me." A smile curved her swollen lips. Her finger curled into the silk string, and his hand clamped down on hers. "Leave it."

They were too damn pretty to be thrown on the floor. He kissed her fast and hard, dragging his mouth down her body to the strip of red. He yanked the silk aside and swiped his tongue along her center. She cried out, body bowing as he added a finger into her slick heat.

She tasted like a sweet dream, her body yielding to his ministrations. He touched his tongue to the swollen bundle of nerves, and her hands smacked the mattress. He swiped once, twice, then sucked, his finger sliding in deep.

Her legs quivered, and her ass wiggled, but he didn't relent. Her fingers curled into the comforter, yanking and tugging until she cried out, body convulsing beneath his mouth. With a smile, he lifted and sheathed himself before plunging deep into her heat.

She cried out again, and he leaned down, capturing her lips and swallowing her cries. He moved in and out of her, pumping with long, deep strokes. He'd fought so hard to live, but he could die right now and not regret a single thing.

Olivia's eyes met his, and he held her gaze as he thrust over and over. Her lips parted, and a moan rumbled up her throat. He dropped his head, taking her nipple in his mouth, nipping and sucking.

He moved his hand beneath her, and in one fluid move he had her on top of him. He slid to the edge of the bed, holding her close, their slick bodies sliding against each other.

Their eyes met in heat and lust, and while that's all Shane wanted to see, he saw much more than that. He saw light and joy, warmth and excitement. He saw a future filled with love and adventure.

He saw long walks on the beach, nights in each other's arms. He saw wedding bells and a picket fence.

And for the first time in his life, he wanted it.

He wanted to believe that his life was different and all of that was possible.

He held her tighter. Her taut nipples dragged along his chest as he pumped into her slick heat. Their mouths found each other in a clash of teeth and tongue, heated desire slamming him in the chest and radiating out from head to toe.

Olivia rocked her hips, taking back control. He was a prisoner to her, willing to sacrifice it all as long as she kept sliding up and down his erection.

Her nails dug into his back, cutting sharp and sending him spiraling toward the edge. He pumped harder, slipping his hand beneath their slick bodies and finding her swollen button. Refusing to fall over the edge without her, he ran his thumb over her clit. Her hips rocked faster, harder, taking him deeper. He clung to his tiny thread of strength.

"Come for me," he said.

Her grip tightened, her body lifting and slamming down, hips thrusting with greedy precision. Her arm trembled, legs shook, and her slick walls tightened around his cock. A scream tore from her mouth, her body convulsing against him. He held her hips and shoved inside her. Pleasure gripped his balls, white lights exploded behind his eyes, and with one final thrust, he spilled his release.

He gathered Olivia in his arms, holding her tight as their jagged breaths became one.

He'd been through hell, a life of more lows than highs, and he'd do it again if it meant he'd wind up right here. Olivia was the light at the end of his very dark tunnel, and even though he swore he'd never give his heart away, he already had.

Olivia had taken control, and now she owned him completely.

He rested his forehead against hers, placing a chaste kiss on her lips. A smile curved her mouth, and she glanced up, looking him straight in the eye. "That was better than I imagined, and I have quite the imagination."

"We'll have to do it again some time," he joked.

"How about now?"

He laid back, taking her with him and tucking her into his side. "I'm going to need a few minutes. You sucked the life out of me."

"I guess we can lay here for a while." She kissed his chest and snuggled into his side.

Her finger traced the imperfection above his pec. His body tensed as her touch traced over the scarred skin.

"What's this from?" she asked.

His port scar—the only visible reminder of his childhood illness. All the other scars were skin deep, unable to be seen by anyone but him. He didn't like being vulnerable, didn't like to admit that at ten years old, he didn't know if he'd make it to twenty-five. But here he was, alive and with a gorgeous woman in his bed. He didn't want to walk down memory lane into the dark depths of the road. He wanted to leave all that shit behind him as he'd been doing.

He didn't believe in looking back. Looking forward was the only way to go. The minute he looked back he'd be reminded of everything he lost.

If he told her the truth, he'd be opening the door for their connection to deepen. He couldn't let that happen. He didn't want to see the sad look in her eyes when he told her about the shitty hand he'd been dealt. Olivia was light, and he didn't want to let his darkness dim her.

He grasped her biceps and flipped her beneath him. That adorable giggle floated out, and he captured her mouth in one fell swoop. All his thoughts silenced, and he let the taste and feel of Olivia take him away.

chapter 17

Olivia sat across from Isla and Harper in a booth at Aunt Greta's diner. She had a few hours before her shift started and called the girls to grab a late breakfast. It was another added benefit of being home. She could call her best friends for an impromptu get together without the hassle of planning around a train schedule.

Harper took a sip of her herbal tea. "Heard Daniel showed up at McConnell's last night."

"According to Maria, Shane almost knocked him out," Isla added.

Olivia laughed at the misinformation caused by a train of gossip going through the town. It was time she set the record straight. "Shane didn't almost knock Daniel out, though I kind of wish he did. Shane didn't even make a fist. He did, however, defend me. I was embarrassed at first by the whole situation, but I don't know… with Shane it's different. Like I can be myself without worrying what he might think. Even if the version of myself is a little messy."

Isla took a bite of her waffle and lifted her chin to Olivia. "But…?"

"What do you mean but?" Olivia asked. There wasn't anything else left to tell.

"You have that look like you want to say more, but you're holding back."

Olivia touched her cheek. "I don't have a look."

Harper all but snorted. "Yes, you do."

Isla's features softened, her porcelain skin radiant and beautiful without a touch of makeup. "We're your best friends. You don't have to worry about what we might think."

"What she said," Harper said around a bite of pancake.

It was silly really, but it had been nagging at her, and maybe talking it out with her friends would help her get some clarity.

She took a sip of her coffee and placed down her mug. "I feel like there's something he's not telling me. He has this scar on his chest, and when I asked him about it, he kissed me instead of answering. I've asked him about his friends, and he always manages to dodge the question. If I could just find out… I don't know. I just want him to be able to open up to me, you know?"

He'd talked about his mom so openly, but there was something he wasn't saying. There were gaps in his story, and it hurt that he didn't trust her enough to share those pieces of himself. Whatever it was that he was holding back, she didn't care. She wouldn't judge him. She just wanted to know so there were no secrets between them.

Isla shook her head and pointed her fork at Olivia. "Oh no. Absolutely not. I tried to be sneaky once and failed miserably at it."

Harper rolled her eyes. "Having a radio station involved isn't exactly sneaky."

Isla flung her fork toward Harper, stabbing the air. "You shush."

"The only person you have to blame is yourself there," Olivia added.

Isla, for whatever reason, thought it was a good idea to set her ex-boyfriend up by a local radio station to catch him cheating. Except the poor guy was as loyal as they come. The fall out was a disaster, and she and Harper had spent many nights helping Isla wipe up tears over margaritas and nachos.

It had been three years since that disastrous day, and Isla insisted she was over Nolan, but nobody believed her—especially since Isla hadn't been on a single date since the breakup.

"We're not talking about me," Isla said. "We're talking about Olivia and her problems."

"You're right," Harper said. "We don't have enough time to talk about your problems. We'd need at least a week."

Isla's head tilted feigning annoyance. "Says the girl who has had more dates in the last month than most people have in a year."

Harper held her hands in front of her, a smile tugging at the corner of her glossed lips. "Hey, I'll be the first to admit that I have a mile-long list of problems, but you're right. This is about Liv." Harper turned toward Olivia. "What do you think it is?" she asked. "I mean what could he possibly be hiding?"

Olivia shrugged.

"Why don't you just ask him?" Isla suggested.

She'd thought about it, but she didn't want to be pushy. "You don't think that's intrusive?"

"He had his penis inside you," Harper said. "You can't get more intrusive than that."

Isla's aquamarine eyes widened. "Are you getting more vulgar with age, or am I just aware of it more now?"

"Probably a combination of both. Then again, when you haven't had sex in as long as you have, everything would sound vulgar."

Isla let out a loud huff. "I'm sorry, unlike you I can't spread my legs for anyone who is ready and willing."

Harper smirked. By the tone in Isla's voice, she was clearly joking. "Hey, I don't spread my legs for just anyone. They have to buy me dinner first."

Olivia choked on her drink. She missed this. She missed being with her best friends and listening to them trade jabs in good fun.

She cleared her throat and tried to steer the conversation back on track. "What do you think I should do?"

"Talk to him," Harper said.

"Let it go," Isla said at the same time.

"I should have known you two would be on totally opposite pages."

Harper tossed her brown hair over her shoulder and took another bite of her pancakes. "Don't listen to her. She hasn't been with a guy in three years."

Isla shot her a look. "And you've dated half the county, none of which have turned into long-term relationships." Isla stuck her tongue out at Harper, and they both laughed.

"You should talk to him," Harper reiterated. "Maybe he

is holding something back, but he doesn't know how to approach the subject. Asking him gives him the opening he might be looking for."

"Or…" Isla held her hand up. "What if it's something you don't want to know, and you can never look at him the same way again?"

"What could he possibly tell me that I'd never look at him the same way again?" Olivia asked, more curious than anything since Isla was known to have a very colorful imagination.

"It could be anything. He believes he was abducted by aliens and is now controlled by them. Or he's a serial killer who killed his way across the country."

Isla definitely didn't disappoint.

Harper's fork halted before reaching her mouth. Her light brown eyebrow lifted, and she turned her gaze to Isla. "I would love to go in your head for one day just to see what the hell goes on in there."

Isla shrugged. "You'd probably go crazy."

Harper laughed. "You're probably right."

Olivia was confident Shane wasn't abducted by aliens or a serial killer. "Shane is not hiding either of those things from me."

Isla took a sip of her tea, eyebrows lifting above the mug. "Or is he?"

Harper shook her head. "Whatever he tells you can't be much worse than what she's thinking, so just ask him."

Olivia still wasn't sure. "I don't want to push."

"Then don't," Harper said. "If he's keeping something

from you, he'll tell you when he's ready." Harper glanced at her phone. "Crap, I got to go. Milo and I told Tom we'd bring him to McConnell's Market to fill out an application."

Tom, Harper's younger brother, loved to tell people God loved him more so he gave him an extra chromosome. Harper was his biggest advocate and had taken care of him most of his life while her mom spent her nights and weekends partying. Ever since he turned nineteen, he'd been begging Harper to help him get a job.

"Wish him luck for me," Isla said.

Olivia had no doubt, he'd get hired. The entire town loved his infectious smile, quick wit, and caring nature. "Tell him I said to turn on his charm." Tom was a flirt who loved to make women laugh.

Harper snickered. "We're trying to get him a job, not a date." Harper tossed down some cash on the table. "That should cover it. Let me know if I'm short."

Olivia picked up the bills and didn't even need to count. "You're more likely over."

Harper waved her hand. "Put it toward the tip then." Harper never liked to shortchange anyone and was always generous with tipping. Olivia suspected it had to do with her mom. Most things that Harper did was to make sure she was nothing like the woman who birthed her.

Harper left, and Olivia placed the money aside. Isla sipped her tea, and Olivia motioned toward her. "How's your grandma been?"

"I saw her yesterday and her spirit's a little down, but other than that, she seems good. I'm going to stop back there a little later today."

"We have to plan that beach day."

"I'll check her doctor appointments and let you know what days are good."

The waitress dropped off the bill. "Whenever you girls are ready. No rush."

Olivia picked up the check. "Thanks, Annabelle."

Annabelle had been a staple at Aunt Greta's, working there morning and afternoon for as long as Olivia could remember. Sitting in Aunt Greta's with Annabelle as her waitress was another blast of the familiar that made Olivia feel right at home.

She and Isla paid the bill and said their goodbyes. Olivia started walking away when she called out to Isla. Isla spun back around, blonde hair whipping around her like a cape.

"I forgot. Hal's playing tonight at McConnell's. You and Harper should come. We can have a couple drinks when I get off my shift."

Isla gave a thumbs up. "Count us in. I'll text Harp."

Olivia waved goodbye and headed to the pub. Her shift didn't start for another hour, but Shane would be there, and after last night, she couldn't wait to see him again. And who knew, if it was a slow day, maybe they could sneak off to the back, and she could show him just how much she missed him.

chapter 18

Hal jumped up and down, sweat dripping down his face, black eye makeup smudged across his cheeks. He was more than halfway through Alice Cooper's entire catalog and didn't seem to be losing any of his energy. The crowd of twenty roared, cheering for an encore.

Shane wrapped his arm around Olivia's waist, and she leaned her head against his chest. Harper, Isla, and Milo threw their arms up on either side of them, screaming their song requests. Shane laughed when Hal pointed at Milo and delved right into *School's Out*. Milo pumped his fists in the air and pretended to air guitar, jumping up and landing in a half split before getting back to his feet. He had been drinking water all night yet had less inhibitions than people who'd downed nothing but beer.

The chorus came, and the entire pub sang along, some hitting God awful notes, but not letting that hold them back.

Connor manned the bar, giving Shane a fifteen-minute break before he had to return to duty. The kitchen was closed, and Olivia was done for the night. Up until a few minutes ago, he'd been watching her dance with her friends, laugh, and sing.

The desire to join them had been stronger than anything he'd ever known. For so long, he'd kept his distance, refusing to let people in, but these people, this town, were wearing him down. He knew he had to be strong, but for one more night, he was letting himself experience life as if he didn't have a care in the world. As if he never had cancer, and he grew up normal, having fun with friends.

He didn't realize the deep-seated ache he had in his heart that was desperate for a connection. It been so long since he had a friend, but looking around now at Connor, Olivia, Milo, Harper, and Isla, he was happy for this time they had together.

Olivia glanced up and kissed his chin. He smiled down at her, holding her tighter. They rocked in sync with the music, and he closed his eyes, absorbing the moment and locking it to memory. If he ever faced death in the face again, he would remember tonight and the sense of normalcy and happiness that filled him with such overwhelming strength.

Hal finished *School's Out,* and Olivia screamed out her request.

"You and Me!"

Hal pointed the microphone at her, sat down on a stool, and swayed as the music played. Milo acted out every line to Harper who laughed at his antics. Olivia turned in Shane's arms, linking her hands behind his neck. Her hips moved in tune with the beat, and his hands slid down to sit firmly on her waist.

She lifted up on tiptoe, pressing a kiss to his lips. He knew he should stop her, knew the entire town was going to have them married off tomorrow and pregnant with twins, but he'd worry about that then. Right now, all he cared about was Olivia's lips on his.

***

Olivia's legs ached from dancing, and her throat hurt from singing along with Hal. Shane managed to keep up with her energy and throughout the night showed small signs of affection—a kiss to the forehead, a squeeze of her hand, a quick tap to the ass when he didn't think anyone would notice.

She didn't want to get her hopes up, but it was hard when Shane had fit in effortlessly with her friends as if he'd been friends with them for years. She still didn't know if Shane was planning on staying or if he was going to up and leave one day. After the time they spent together, she hoped he wouldn't leave.

She made herself at home on his couch while he grabbed a couple of waters for them. She wondered what his place looked like back in California. This house came already furnished, so she couldn't get a glimpse into his own personal style.

Shane came into the room with two glasses and placed them on the coffee table. "I was hoping I'd come in with you naked and waiting."

"Is that so?" She grasped his hand and yanked him on to the couch with her. "I'm sorry to disappoint you."

He kissed her, soft and sweet. "You could never disappoint me."

"Give me time," she joked.

He tickled her side, and she let out a yelp as she curved her body to dodge his fingers. He got her on the other side, and she wiggled against him, but he managed to flip her beneath him, pinning her down with his solid frame.

Laughs poured out of her, the torture turning her on. She twisted and turned, but he was relentless. A smirk settled on her face as she reached down and grabbed his dick through his pants. His entire body froze, and she smiled in victory.

She rubbed, running her thumb up and down his hardened length. She bit her lip, loving how she could stop him in his tracks. The control turned her on, made her feel strong and desired.

Moisture pooled between her legs as she pulled the zipper down and released him. His erection stood at attention; an impressive sight of flesh attached to an impressive man. The night she had met Shane, she thought she was done with men. She didn't think she'd be capable of picking up the pieces and opening her heart to someone else.

From the night she met him, without him even realizing, he gathered the shattered pieces of her heart, and not only put them back together, but made them stronger. He made her feel powerful at a time when she had never felt weaker. He lifted her up in spirit and in nature, making her feel special despite all her tribulations.

She shifted to get on her knees and show Shane exactly how much she appreciated him, but before she could, he flipped her beneath him, his hardness pressing firmly against her center. "I've been thinking about this all night." He dipped his head, devouring her in a searing kiss that shot fire through her veins.

Her insides melted as his hands roamed her body. The warmth of his finger touched her stomach and trailed a line to the waist of her pants. A frantic need ripped through her and she fumbled with her button, pushing her pants down, desperate for his touch.

Shane helped her, pulling her legs free of the restricting material. His mouth traveled down her neck, sucking on the sensitive skin at the crook. Desire spiraled with need and she shoved at his pants. She didn't want anything between them. All she wanted was their bare bodies, uninhibited, free of barriers, sliding against each other.

He reached behind him, pulling his shirt over his head and she followed suit. She unhooked her bra and quickly tossed it in the pile of clothes on the floor. Her fingers trailed up and down the cut lines of his chest.

The sound of foil ripping echoed through the quiet house. Olivia squirmed as she patiently waited for Shane. An all-consuming need so potent, so intense overwhelmed her. Her body ached for more, craved the only thing that Shane could give her.

Finally, his strong hand cupped her ass, angling her body. She lifted, opening her thighs to him, tossing her inhibitions to the night. In one quick thrust he entered her. She cried out as soft tissue stretched to accommodate him. Her muscles clenched around him, and her head fell back, eyes rolled toward the ceiling as a million explosions detonated through her body, fueling an inferno of heat and pleasure.

She grabbed his face, bringing his mouth to hers,

desperate to be as close to him as possible. Needing to be connected in every way possible. Their tongues thrashed and slid, bodies rocked and bucked until they moved as one. Shane's thumb found her clit and with a gentle stroke, her body tightened with built up pleasure. He pumped into her, his thumb moving in delicious strokes, propelling her toward release.

She dug her fingers into the hard flesh of his ass, urging him to go harder, faster. She relaxed, absorbing every stroke, every sensual touch of his hands and mouth.

White hot heat flashed, her body tightened, preparing for the release. With one final thrust, she exploded, screaming out Shane's name. A feeling washed over her in a wave of intensity, knocking her world upside down, drowning her in complete and total bliss. She savored the sensations devouring her body, opening herself and her heart up and letting Shane in completely.

She opened her eyes, locking with his as realization settled over her.

Somehow, someway, she'd fallen in love with the boy from the train.

***

The next morning, Shane's phone buzzed, and he reluctantly left Olivia's naked body. He swiped his phone off the nightstand, rubbed the sleep from his eyes, and focused on the screen. A new text from Mimi popped up. He opened the text and read.

She was inviting him to a family dinner at the house. He'd met all his family, at least those that lived in Morgan's

Bay, but he had never experienced them all together.

Would the dynamic be different? He couldn't say no, but he didn't want to go alone either.

He texted back.

Can I bring a friend?

Of course!

Shane put his phone down and snaked an arm around Olivia's waist. "Would you like to come to Bayview for dinner tonight?"

Olivia's eyes widened. "To Bayview? I have nothing to wear! All my good clothes are in the city, and I told Daniel I didn't want any of them." She sat up a look of panic on her face. "I need to go shopping."

Shane lay down and pulled Olivia with him. Her body flopped over his, and he angled toward her. "You do not need to go shopping. It's just dinner. Nothing fancy."

"It's dinner at Bayview Estate with your grandparents who basically own the entire town. How can I not go shopping?"

"One, because you don't need to spend the money." He kissed her forehead, and she sighed her disappointment to the truth in his statement. "And two, you don't have to impress anyone with your clothes. You do that with your intelligence, charm, and kindness."

"You're just looking for brownie points," she said.

"And you're digging for me to keep going with the compliments."

She pressed her lips together, eyes rolling upward, smirk tugging at the edge of her mouth. "I would never."

He kissed the corner of her mouth. "Liar."

A glint of silver caught Shane's attention. He rolled toward it, and Olivia rested her chin on his shoulder. "What are you looking at?" He kissed her forehead then threw his feet over the bed and walked toward the dull metal.

He bent down and picked it up, placing the ring in the palm of his hand. His heart slammed in his chest as the familiar inscription looked back at him. *How was that even possible?*

"What is it?" Olivia sat up on the bed and tucked the sheet around her.

He held the ring up. It had been years since he'd seen this ring, but he'd never forget what it looked like.

"Probably from the previous tenant," she said.

"No," Shane stared at the inscription as he backed up to the bed and sat. "This is my mother's ring."

Olivia moved closer, looking at the ring in his hand. "Are you sure?"

"I'm positive. My dad gave her this ring. She wore it all the time, but she lost it."

"How did it get here?"

"That's a really good question." Shane stood up and pulled his pants on. "And I'm going to find out tonight."

"Do you think your mom was here?"

"I don't know. Every time I think I have this screwed up puzzle figured out a new piece presents itself and brings me back to square one."

chapter 19

Shane put the car in park and took a deep breath before getting out. Olivia was out before he made it to her side of the car, but she let him close the door. "And here I thought chivalry was dead," she joked.

Shane took her hand and squeezed. "I'm just trying to impress you."

"Consider me impressed."

"Hey." He tugged on her hand, and she stopped, turning to him.

"What's up?" she asked.

"I know you wanted to handle Daniel on your own, and I never apologized for jumping in like I did."

"You have nothing to be sorry about. I didn't mind the assist. I was grateful for it."

"I was happy to, but I also need you to know that I did it for my own selfish reasons, not because I didn't' think you were capable."

A knowing smile lit her face. "I know. Now, are you done stalling?"

Shane laughed and kissed her knuckles. "That obvious?"

"Your hand is a little sweaty," she joked.

He let go of her hand and wiped his palm on his pants. She immediately reached out and laced her fingers through his. "If I knew you were going to drop my hand, I wouldn't have said anything."

He smiled, and she could see it was for her as it was as much for him.

"You've already met everyone."

"I know, but I met them all separately. Now they're all going to be together at one table."

"Everything will be fine."

"I hope so."

Shane led the way up the front steps and knocked on the door. Connor opened the door, and Olivia relaxed at the familiar face. He swooped down and hugged her, then motioned them inside.

Olivia stepped into the McConnell house—the house she dreamed about living in since she was a little child. It was an open floor plan with big windows throughout, showcasing the amazing views of the bay. The walls weren't lined with gold gilt like she'd assumed they would be. Instead, white crown molding framed the room. The walls were a beautiful shade of yellow that brightened the entire house and were complimented by navy, yellow, and white accents that looked like a photoshoot for a high-class magazine.

While it was unbelievably pretty, it felt void of life. There were no scratches on the floor, scuffs on the coffee table, or wear on the upholstery.

Her whole life she couldn't appreciate what she had, too focused on what she didn't have. If she would have taken a moment to realize, she would have realized that there was nothing wrong with her life. She'd had blinders on for so long, and they were finally falling away and revealing the things she should have seen all along. Money didn't buy happiness.

"Shane, darling." His grandmother came into the room, arms up, martini dangling from one hand. She took Shane in a hug and turned her attention to Olivia.

Shane placed a hand on Olivia's lower back. "Mimi, this is Olivia Green."

"It's a pleasure to meet you."

"You have a lovely home, Mrs. McConnell. Thank you for having me."

"Please, call me, Mimi. Everyone else does."

Olivia felt honored to be able to refer to this woman she had idolized for so long in such a personal manner.

"Come, come. We're all sitting outside on the patio for cocktails." Shane's shoulders set in a rigid tense angle and his head bent up at tight attention.   Olivia squeezed Shane's hand as they followed Mimi to the backyard, hoping to calm whatever was going on in his mind.

"Shane," Morgan's Bay mayor—Shane's uncle—stood from an Adirondack chair and came over to greet them. He shook Shane's hand and pulled him into a hug. Shane hesitated, awkwardly patting his uncle on the back. Olivia had thought Shane liked his uncle, so why was he so closed off?

Mayor McConnell smiled at Olivia, and Shane once again placed his hand on her lower back. "Uncle Grady, this is Olivia Green."

"Are you Rick's kid?" he asked.

"I am."

"He's a good man, your father. Always keeps me on my toes at the town meetings."

Olivia could only imagine. "He is strong in his beliefs."

"Tell him I say hi and look forward to the next meeting. We'll be discussing the geese issue on the football field and track. I'm sure he'll have plenty to contribute."

Dad had been complaining about the geese since she was in school after he was chased off the track by a very aggressive mama goose. Every spring he was driven out of his daily track laps after school because the geese took up residency. "I wish you all the luck with that one."

Connor joined them few minutes later, and Olivia wondered if Mr. McConnell himself would show up. Connor instantly fell into roll of bartender, mixing drinks for everyone and laughing when Mimi tested his knowledge on basic mixology. He aced all the questions she threw his way.

The elegant society woman Olivia envied and always wanted to be turned out to be a woman who loved her family. Being with her family, laughing with them, put an extra twinkle in her blue eyes. Her smile had nothing to do with the big house, the amazing view, or the designer glasses she drank from. It was her family.

Olivia couldn't believe how wrong she had been. She didn't need money to be happy. Everything she needed to be happy, she already had.

The tension in the air shifted, and Olivia turned just as the patriarch himself stepped onto the patio. "Are we eating or what? I have a conference call in an hour."

Mimi grabbed her martini glass and shuffled toward the door. She kissed Mr. McConnell on the cheek. "Olivia, darling, come help me. Let the men fraternize."

Shane squeezed her hand, and she headed toward the door.

"I have work to do. Call me when dinner is ready." Mr. McConnell went back inside and disappeared down the hall.

"He's always so busy." Mimi waved her hand in his direction like she was used to making excuses for his departures.

"What's left to cook?" Olivia asked, hoping it was something she could handle.

"Oh sweetie, I don't cook. But I'm a pro at calling for takeout. We just have to empty the containers onto serving plates."

"I like your style," Olivia said.

"Stick around, darling, and I'll teach you all my tricks."

The thought warmed Olivia's heart. She didn't even care anymore about the McConnell name and what it represented. Just the idea of being a part of Shane's family was enough for her.

***

Grandfather, as Shane learned he liked to be called, finally joined them at the table. Shane couldn't help but wonder if he was the reason Grandfather had stuck to his office. God forbid he opened himself up for dialogue.

Shane moved his food around his plate. It was all delicious, but his appetite was nonexistent.

The ring weighed heavy in his pocket. He had so many

questions, and the only people who could answer any of those questions were at this very table. Someone had information, knew something that he didn't, and it was time that he knew. He slipped the ring from his pocket and rolled it between his fingers.

There was a pause in conversation, and he decided it was now or never. "I found this at the house I'm staying at." He held up Mom's long missing ring.

"Must be from one of the past tenants," Mimi said.

"Except it's not," Shane said. "It's my mothers."

Mimi's eyebrows fought the Botox and rose. "That's not possible."

"I didn't think so either. She wore this ring every day. Only took it off to put lotion on her hands. It was given to her by my father the night before he died."

"I'm sure there are thousands of rings that look like that," Grandfather said. "It's just a coincidence."

"I thought so too. Except for the inscription. My father proposed by giving my mom this ring and pointing to these words." Shane looked at the inscription and read it aloud. "*Forever you and me.* It was then she told him she was pregnant with me. It was the happiest day of Mom's life other than when I was born. And I know this because she told me. Because she never took this damn ring off. Until one day after I was in the hospital, and she told me she had to go away for a few days, but not to worry, she'd be back soon. And when she came back, the ring was gone. She never told me where she went, but now I know. She came here."

Every expression at the table filled with shock except

for a select few. Those few knew something. They were keeping secrets, and Shane was done tiptoeing around. He wanted answers, and damn it, he was going to get them.

"Tell me I'm wrong," Shane said. "Tell me this is all just some crazy coincidence, and my mother's ring just magically appeared."

"She was here," Uncle Grady said, and Shane's attention snapped to him.

"How do you know?" Grandfather asked, voice steady and unwavering, but Shane could see the flicker of shock in his eyes.

"I heard you two the day she showed up on the doorstep. Mom was at one of her luncheons. It was raining, and you were waiting for a call from your investor. I came by to talk about the bar, but when I had seen the mood you were in, I thought better of it. I ran upstairs to grab something out of my old room. I don't even remember what anymore, but that's not important anyway. When I was coming back down, I saw you at the door with her. She was drenched, hair hanging down, dripping on the threshold. You wouldn't even let her in out of the rain. She told you who she was, and you denied her—told her to get off the property and never come back. I was curious, so I went after her."

Olivia's hand landed on Shane's thigh, and he gripped her hand like a lifeline as his uncle continued.

"You didn't believe her, but there was something in my gut that told me I needed to find out myself. She didn't have a car—must've had a cab drop her off—so it was easy to catch up to her. I convinced her to let me give her a ride, and she told me everything. And I believed her. She knew things about my brother that no one else would."

"So, you just let her go?" Shane didn't even attempt to hide the anger and frustration in his tone. His hand came free of Olivia's, and he shot up from his chair.

"No." Uncle Grady met his eyes. "She was desperate to get back to you, but she was wet and tired. I could see the exhaustion consuming her. She'd been going on adrenaline, and she was crashing, so I took her to the rental. It was vacant at the time. I told her to get some sleep, and I'd send car service to pick her up early in the morning before the neighbors would be up and snooping out their windows. She must've dropped the ring then. I'm surprised in all these years, no one had found it."

"It was wedged in a crack between floorboards."

Uncle Grady nodded.

"So, you gave her a place to crash, and then you dismissed her, too?" Shane asked. It was a shame he was starting to like Uncle Grady.

Uncle Grady shook his head. "No. I wrote her a check for ten thousand dollars and gave her my personal phone number in case she ever needed anything else. I told her never hesitate to call."

Shane remembered that trip. Remembered when Mom returned and how she suddenly didn't seem like the entire world was pressing in on her. She had a softness to her smile, a lighter demeanor overall. The money helped but… "You gave her hush money."

"It wasn't like that," Uncle Grady said.

"No? Then why is it that I didn't know you existed until a few months ago? Why didn't you go to him?" Shane flung his hand out and pointed a stern finger at Grandfather. "Convince him that I was his grandson. If you believed it then why keep me secret?"

"I was young," Uncle Grady said. "Just about your age now. I hadn't come into all the money in my trust, and I was afraid to lose it. Thinking back, I realize how selfish that was, but I didn't think then the way I do now. But I kept in touch with your mother.

She never accepted money from me after that, but I still sent her things. Gift cards mostly. After she died… I had no way of knowing where you were or if you were still healthy. Which is why last month I had hired a private investigator to find you. You showed up here before he found you."

Shane stared at Uncle Grady in disbelief. All this time, he believed he had no family other than his mother. And all along he had an extended family. His uncle had looked out for him just as family was supposed to.

"Why didn't you ever tell me this?" Mimi demanded from Grandfather.

Grandfather sighed and dropped his fork. "She came here that one time. Took me by surprise. I have a temper; we all know that. By the time I calmed down and could think rationally, she was long gone. I had no address, no contact information. There was nothing I could do."

"But she sent you a letter. I saw it in your office," Connor said, tossing his napkin on the table.

Uncle Grady looked at his son. "Wait a second, you knew?"

"I didn't know if it was true. Thought maybe it was someone trying to swindle money out of Grandfather. Until Shane showed up. Look at him. There's no denying he's a McConnell. That he's Uncle Shane's son. I've seen pictures. His complexion is darker, but come on… same eyes."

"What letter?" Mimi asked. The confusion in her brow told Shane she knew as little about the letter as he did.

Even after being cast aside by this man, Mom reached out again. Shane knew the strength and desperation she must have felt in order to do so.

"Where's the letter?" Shane asked. Grandfather didn't budge, his stature rigid as ever, eyes cast forward, blank and emotionless as usual. "I want to see it." When he didn't respond, anger surged through Shane, and he slammed his fist down on the table. Plates jumped and clattered, glasses nearly tipped over, and Olivia beside him diverted her gaze to her lap. He should have given her shoulder a reassuring squeeze, but he was too angry right now.

Mimi leaned in her chair, arms crossed over her chest. "I'd like to see this letter, too."

"Oh, all right," Grandfather growled and stormed out of the dining room.

Tension filled the large space, making it impossible to breathe comfortably, but Shane didn't care. He'd gone his whole life not knowing these people even existed, yet they knew he did. His mother reached out more than once, and they didn't care. At least Grandfather. Uncle Grady did the best he could, and for that, Shane would forever be indebted to him.

"Here." Grandfather handed him a folded piece of paper.

Shane reluctantly took the letter in hand and unfolded it. The familiar handwriting punched at his heart, and he held back a stinging sadness that burned his throat.

I write to you now as a mother about to leave her only child in the world with little to no family. Other than my uncle in Portugal, Shane has no family to speak of—except that he does. He has an entire family he doesn't know exists…an entire family who doesn't know he exists. It is my dying wish that you push aside whatever malice you have in your heart toward me and open your arms to your grandson. Give him the family he could have only dreamed of, a chance to get to know you, the mother of the father he never met. Share with him stories I couldn't because I simply didn't know. Share your love because he will share it right back.

He is a man now, and with each day he grows more and more like his father in not only his appearance, but in his mannerisms, his kind heart, and his love of adventure. Shane is the greatest gift given to me by your son before his untimely passing, and now I hope I can share that gift with you.

As my days near their end, I can't help but to reflect on the past and question so many choices, conversations, everything really. I'm sorry I couldn't have gotten to know you. I honestly think we would have gotten along. Maybe even liked each other. If only things were different. If only Shane didn't leave us so soon.

I can't do anything about the past, but I can do something about the future. Which is why I beg you… Don't leave my son without a family.

   Truly Yours,

   Aurora Sanchez

Tears pressed at the back of his eyes; heat filled his lungs and clogged his throat. Even on her deathbed she worried about him. By the date at the top of the letter, she'd written this less than a week before she died. She knew she didn't have much longer to live, yet she took that precious time and did what she always did. She tried to make sure he wasn't alone in life.

His lip quivered, and he dropped the letter on the table. His eyes met Grandfather's, and he spun away from him and headed to the door. He stopped midway and turned back to the man that denied him for so long. "All she ever wanted from you was for you to believe her. For you to reach beyond the blackness in your heart and accept me. It's no wonder my father left. I wouldn't want to be around a miserable, selfish prick either."

Grandfather glared at him, hard lines cutting deep into the sides of his mouth, showing his deteriorating age. "How dare you speak to me like that in my own home."

"And that's your problem. You're up so high and mighty on your goddamn thrown that no one can say or do anything. Everyone tiptoes around here, so they don't upset you. Well, thanks to you I'm not a McConnell, so I don't give a shit what you say or do to me. I've already lost everything. I have nothing left."

"You're just like your father," he barked.

The corner of Shane's mouth tilted. "I know you mean

that as an insult, but it's the only nice thing you've ever said to me. I'll be out of the house tomorrow."

Shane stormed out of the dining room, unable to look at that man for another second.

<h1 style="text-align:center">chapter 20</h1>

Olivia shifted awkwardly in her chair before jumping up to go after Shane. He was so upset, but on top of that, she had questions of her own. *Hospital. Health.*

She stopped and faced Mimi. "Thank you for a lovely dinner."

"Oh sweetie, who are you fooling? This was a goddamn shitshow." Mimi downed the rest of her martini and slammed her glass down on the table.

"I still appreciate the invitation." Despite everything, Olivia still couldn't believe she'd finally stepped foot in the elusive Bayview Estate.

Mimi pushed up from her chair, glared at her husband and stormed out of the room. Olivia smiled to the rest of the table and saw herself out. To think all this time, she considered these people the ultimate dream. In reality, they were filled with secrets and without even realizing it, or maybe they did, they were slowly destroying their family.

Olivia might not have grown up in the big house on the bay, and they might not have owned more than half the town, but her family—as intrusive as they were—would never act toward one another as the McConnells did. They didn't keep secrets from each other. Her father never spoke about Shane's father, but only because it pained him too much. The minute Olivia asked him, he told her everything. Despite his own reservations, he told her.

Olivia headed for the door in a hurry to get to Shane and make sure he was okay. Grady McConnell met her at the door.

"Don't let him leave," he said. "I just got my nephew back, and I don't want to lose him."

Olivia squared her shoulders. "Maybe you should have thought about that years ago. If he leaves that's his decision, not mine."

"Do you not want him to stay?"

What kind of question was that? She'd fallen in love with Shane, but she didn't want him to feel obligated to stay. She already allowed one man to stay in her life out of an obligation. Though it wasn't as much for her as it was for his career, it still was an obligation no less. If Shane was to stay in Morgan's Bay that had to be his decision.

"Of course I do. But I also know what it was like to stay in a situation because I was convinced it was the only way to be happy. Because on the surface that was exactly what it seemed, but if I'd just opened my damn eyes for two seconds, I would've realized I wasn't happy. Not at all. And I don't want that for Shane. I want him to make his own choices. I don't want to guilt him in to staying. I want him to stay because he simply wants to stay. I can't make that choice for him and neither can you."

He rested his hand on her shoulder, an empathetic sadness in his green eyes. "I understand. Still, he needs you right now. Go to him."

Olivia had every intention of doing just that. She gave Mayor McConnell a nod and hurried out of the house.

She found Shane sitting on the bumper of his car. She went to him, and he looked up at her with such pain in his eyes. "I'm sorry I left you in there." His voice cracked, and his head bowed, pressing against her stomach. She held him, hugging his head to her and assured him it was okay.

"Hey." She rested her hand on his chin. "Look at me."

He glanced up, brownish green eyes locking on hers.

"You okay?"

"I don't know."

She reached into his pocket, and his eyebrow arched. She grabbed his keys and pulled them out. "Let's get out of here."

"After everything that just went down, you don't want to bolt?"

"Why would I?"

"My family is a dysfunctional mess."

"Last Thanksgiving my sister locked herself in the bathroom for an hour because my dad made a joke about her forehead wrinkle. My dad also wears monster slippers, and my parents ride a golf cart around town. We all have our fair share of crazy." She kissed his forehead like he'd done to her so many times. She'd found it comforting, and she hoped it had the same effect on him. "Come on. Let's get out of here."

She got in the driver seat, turned the car on, and pulled out of the long driveway. Unsure of where to go, she headed toward the beach. "Want to talk about it?"

Shane kept his eyes on the road in front of them. "I don't know."

Olivia always felt better when she could talk things out, but Shane was different. He didn't wear his emotions on his sleeve for everyone to see like she did.

He snapped at dinner, but it wasn't enough. He ran out before any real healing words could be spewed from his mouth. She almost wanted to bring him back, so he could finish. Cutting himself open and bleeding the thoughts and insecurities he'd been feeling for a while would rid him of the poison.

She turned down a side street and drove toward his place instead. It had become their sanctuary away from the outside world. She didn't know what to say, so she waited for him to speak, but he never did. She pulled into the driveway and put the car in park.

They went into the house in silence. Olivia wanted to say something. Anything. There was so much that had happened, but the thing that stuck out to her the most was what his uncle had said to him. "What did your uncle mean by not knowing if you were still healthy?"

The skin on the bridge of his nose wrinkled. "It was nothing. I'm sure."

It was something, though. She saw the concern in his uncle's eyes, and she knew whatever it was, it was the missing piece. It was the thing he was keeping from her. Harper had told her just to ask him, and she didn't think she could. Figured he would tell her when he was ready. But she'd waited long enough.

"Why do I feel like you're not telling me something?"

His body tensed, shoulders rigid and eyes flashing

annoyance. "What are you talking about?"

"I don't know, Shane. I ask you about your friends in California, and you either change the subject or distract me with kisses. You talk about your mom, but I feel like there's a huge chunk of your life missing. Is it something you're ashamed of? Because I don't care. I don't care whatever it is because…I love you."

***

Shane stumbled back at her admission. She loved him. Nobody other than his mom ever loved him. He wouldn't let them. People got close, and he hurt them. He couldn't do that to Olivia. She was everything that was good in the world, and he wouldn't take that away from her.

Her eyes locked on his, hopeful yet scared. All he had to do was admit the truth. Tell her that he loved her, too. But he couldn't. She deserved a future to look forward to, and he had no idea what his future held. For all he knew, he could live to be a senior citizen, never relapsing, and being healthy, strong. But what if he wasn't so lucky? What if he got sick again? He refused to subject Olivia to that life. He watched Mom waste her days in sadness, never finding happiness after losing the love of her life. Then with what little time she had left, she gave it away to stay in a hospital with him.

Olivia couldn't love him.

"Don't say that," he said.

"Say what?" Her eyes filled with hurt. "That I love you? I'm not taking it back."

God she was feisty and strong willed. And damn it to

hell, he did love her. He loved her more than he loved anyone before. He couldn't imagine a day when he didn't get to see that beautiful smile or hear her adorable giggle that flooded him with joy. But could he give her a life that she wanted?

Mom sacrificed her life for him, spending her days at doctor appointments and in hospital rooms. Then finally, when he was healthy and she could go back to her life, making up for all the lost time, she got sick. She didn't win the battle. She lost, and in the end, her to-do list was left unchecked.

Shane couldn't expect Olivia to sacrifice her life for him if it came to that. And even if she was able to, there was a possibility that he couldn't have children. Infertility wasn't uncommon in children who went through chemo and radiation. What if he stayed and she wanted a family, and he couldn't give her that?

The only thing he'd be bringing to a relationship was uncertainty.

He met her gaze, brown eyes filled with such sorrow it damn near broke his heart. "Loving me is a mistake."

"Why?" She practically begged, but he still couldn't bring himself to tell her the truth, and maybe that made him a coward. "Just tell me?"

Anger at the shitty hand of life he was dealt swelled inside him. He bit back the rage.

"Please." Her words were a mere whisper, but the impact was hard and intense.

"Because!" His temper got the better of him. The word

cut through the air like a wrecking ball, knocking Olivia back and leaving her wide eyed and stunned. He ripped his shirt down, revealing his scar.

"You want to know what this is?" he asked.

"Yes." Her voice was small, too small.

"This is a scar from a port—a device that was placed under my skin so I could receive chemo."

Her lips parted, and her eyes filled with disbelief. "Chemo? Are you… are you dying?" she asked, pain filling her tone. And that right there was exactly why he couldn't drag her into his life.

"I beat it, but that doesn't mean it can't come back in some form or another."

Moisture pooled in her eyes, and he could see the pity forming. She reached out to him, but he didn't want her comfort. He didn't want her to feel bad for him. He fought and he won. And he would continue fighting, but it was his battle, not hers.

He stepped back, and her hand fell limply to her side. He slipped out his phone and tapped his screen before sliding his phone back in his pocket.

"I can't do this," he said.

"Do what?"

"Stand here and let you feel sorry for me."

"I…"

"It's okay. I get it. Comes with the territory."

"Can't we just talk about this?"

He didn't want to talk. She'd just try to justify everything, and he didn't want to be the one to burst her bubble. There was no justifying anything. People lived and they died, and when he allowed himself to get attached, all that followed was heartache and misery. "There's nothing to talk about. You know everything now."

"So, you finally open up to me and that's it? You want nothing to do with me now?"

He didn't want to look at her, but he needed to be firm in his stance. "It's for the best."

"That's a fucking lie and you know it." A tear fell from her lid and she swatted it away. "I thought you were different. I thought that you saw me for me."

"I do." He saw her for exactly who she was. He'd watch her grow from that blubbering mess on the train to a strong, confident woman who wasn't afraid of anything. It was because of that, he couldn't stay.

"No, you don't. If you truly saw me, knew me, you would know that what I see when I look at you is not pity. I see a man who has been through hell and fought like a beast to be where he is now. I see a man who is incapable of letting people in, so he uses his past illness as a scapegoat. You've been fighting your whole life, and now you just want to give up." She straightened, thrusting her shoulders back. "That's fine. I deserve better. I deserve a man who will fight for me."

Her words hit him square in the gut, knocking the wind out of him. The sadness etched into the sides of her eyes and corner of her mouth was like tiny knives to his heart. He resisted the urge to go to her. He never wanted this.

He was supposed to be the rebound. The girl didn't fall

in love with the rebound.

His lips parted, but like a sign from above, a horn blared outside.

"What's that?" she asked,

"Your ride. Tell Milo, thanks."

With that, Shane walked away from Olivia. He thought he made the right choice, but as he shut the bedroom door and collapsed on the bed, he couldn't help but wonder if she was right.

Had he given up?

chapter 21

Shane stood behind the bar, and for the first time since he came to Morgan's Bay, he felt like he didn't belong. Between the complete blow up with his family then the fight with Olivia, he was feeling out of sorts. He'd be out of here soon; he just didn't want to leave Connor shorthanded.

Connor smacked him on the back. "You certainly know how to make an impression."

"About that…" Shane started, but Connor held his hand up.

"No need to apologize. If you ask me, I think you held yourself back. I would have been furious. So, don't sweat it. Honestly."

Connor was kind to say so, but guilt still tugged at Shane's gut. "I came here because I wanted a family. Instead, I singlehandedly destroyed one."

"No," Connor said. "You can't destroy something that was already falling apart. This family has been holding itself together with tape for so long. We all knew it wouldn't hold forever. That's not on you, so don't think it is."

"It's hard not to."

"If you ask me, you've done this family a favor. It's about time we stop hiding behind false pretenses and face reality. Especially Grandfather. You're the first person to stand up to him the way you did, and trust me, we're all grateful for it."

"How's Mimi?" Shane still felt awful for being the one to drop the bomb that her husband had been keeping a secret from her for years.

"Mimi is resilient. You don't have to worry about her."

The door opened, sun shining in from outside and surrounding Olivia as she made her way in. She looked like a damn angel, and Shane had to look away before he was blinded by her light.

"Hey, Liv!" Connor called out. He patted Shane's shoulder. "I'll leave you two alone."

Shane dropped his head and turned toward the condiment tray, grabbing a jar of cherries.

"Uh oh. Trouble in paradise?" Connor asked.

"I don't want to talk about it."

"Word of cousinly advice… Last night was the perfect example of what happens when you don't talk. Talking is sometimes the most important thing we have." Connor left for the kitchen, leaving his words to run through Shane's mind.

Shane filled the rest of the tray and looked up. Olivia had put her bag down and tied her apron to her waist. She was in sneakers, a pair of shorts that showed off her sculpted legs, and a t-shirt that clung to her chest. Her brown hair was tousled and reminded him of how it looked fanned around her on his bed.

She was so damn beautiful it hurt. But what hurt even more was that he missed her. He missed her voice, her laugh, her touch, everything about her. Waking up without her beside him was the worst reality check of his life. He almost hoped it had all been a bad dream.

Afternoon slipped into night, and Olivia had uttered only two words to him. *Pinot*, regarding him asking what white her customer wanted, and *lemon*, when he forgot to put a wedge in a diet soda.

This was exactly what he wanted, but now that he had it, he wasn't so sure. His eyes lingered on her as she went from one table to the next. She bent over, picking up a napkin she dropped, and he nearly lost his mind.

He excused himself to the bathroom before he couldn't resist jumping over the bar and crashing his mouth to hers. Inside the bathroom, he threw cold water on his face. He looked up, catching his reflection. The light that he felt spark whenever he was with Olivia was gone, leaving his eyes lifeless and dull.

With a deep breath, he opened the door and went to head out when a hand slammed into his chest and forced him into the single bathroom. Olivia had fire in her eyes and determination in her stance.

"What are you doing?" he asked, resisting the urge to bend down and kiss her.

"I don't know," she admitted. "I had this vision that I would push you in here, and we'd reach for each other, stripping our clothes off. I guess I was wrong."

His cock throbbed at the visual she created. He stood his ground, trying to be strong, but her fruity floral scent floated around him, drowning him in the mouth-watering aroma.

She shifted from one foot to the other, the lack of

confidence in her demeanor showing in the way she fidgeted with her hands. He wanted to assure her that everything would be okay, but he couldn't do that. It was the uncertainty that killed him. Dating him was like a game of Russian roulette, and the chance was too great for him to let her take.

She pinned him with her deep brown gaze. "I just don't understand, and that's what hurts the most. I thought what we had was special. Something to fight for."

"It was special." It was so special, and he would remember every second of their time together. "But you and I both know that I was your rebound." If he could convince her, maybe he'd believe it himself.

She shook her head. "You were so much more than that."

"You think I was, but in a few months, you'll realize I was just the guy who helped you get over your ex. And I'm okay with that."

"Well, I'm not!" She shoved at his chest, and his back hit the sink. Pain radiated up his spine, but it had nothing on the pain in his heart.

She blinked up at him, and his resolve waned. He snaked his hand around her waist and yanked her to him. Their mouths met in frenzied passion, and Shane was too weak to pull away. He thrust his tongue into Olivia's mouth, grabbing her hair and tilting her head for a better angle.

She met his thrust with her own, their tongues a tangled mess of heartache and need. He loved this woman, and he couldn't be weak for her. He reached deep for the strength to push her away, but it was right out of his grasp.

Her fingers dug into his back, and he lifted her, planting her ass on the sink. Her heel pushed into his back, forcing him closer. Her perfect breasts pressed against his chest. The vision of her pert pink nipples was a sweet, sweet memory. All he had to do was reach for the hem of her shirt, and he could relieve every perfect inch of her.

But fear of what he couldn't change or control grabbed him by the throat. That strength that was out of his reach suddenly was close enough to seize.

He ran his hands up her arms, savoring the feel of her one last time, before tightening his grip and stepping back. "This is a mistake."

The disappointment in Olivia's eyes was the equivalent to a direct kick to the balls. She slid off the sink, adjusted her clothes, and ran a finger along her mouth. She nodded and went to walk out when she stopped, turning to face him. "Why don't you stop lying to me now and be honest."

***

There was no way in hell she was walking out of this bathroom without answers. He didn't get to kiss her like that and then declare it was a mistake.

How could he want to deny himself what they had? Why was he punishing them? She waited for his answer, needing to know what it was that was making him run from them.

His chin fell to his chest, and he sighed. "I lived a good portion of my life in and out of hospitals, and I would never wish that life on anyone. I watched my mom give everything up for me, and when she was finally free of taking care of me, she got sick and died. She lost her life for me. If I get sick again, I couldn't expect you to live that life."

Unbelievable. He wouldn't even let her make that choice on her own. "I have no say in any of this?"

"It's for the best."

"That's a load of crap and you know it. You're scared. And I get that, but I'm willing to take that risk. I love you."

A spark lit his eyes, and she felt like she was finally getting through to him. She needed him to see that she didn't care about any of it. All she cared about was having him in her life.

"And will you still love me if I have wires hooked up to my nose and mouth? Will you love me if the chemo makes me so sick, I don't even have the strength to get out of bed to throw up? Will you love me then?"

The thought of seeing strong and healthy Shane, weak and sick unable to get out of bed hurt her heart. She sucked in a breath at the awful thought of Shane being crippled by a horrible disease.

"That's what I thought." Shane spun toward the door and sidestepped her.

"No, that's not what…"

It was too late. He was already gone.

chapter 22

Shane tossed what little clothes he had into his duffel bag. He had no idea where he was going, but he couldn't stay in Morgan's Bay. He'd ruined everything that was good about this place, and he couldn't stick around and see Olivia every single day. He didn't need the reminder that he let go of the best thing that had ever happened to him.

He could call her, go to her, beg her to forgive him, but she was right. He was scared. Scared of repeating the past and watching another person sacrifice everything for him. Nobody was worth that sacrifice, and he couldn't let her think he was.

He looked around the house that had become a home in such a short time. He'd miss the stability and the comfort of the walls. He'd miss the nights when Olivia was curled up in his arms and he fell asleep, knowing she'd be the first person he saw when he woke.

He heard a car door, and his heart skipped a beat. *Stupid.* Even if it was Olivia, he had to be strong. A strong knock echoed through the house, and Shane went to the door. Shock rattled his insides as he stared back at the last person he ever imagined seeing again.

Grandfather stood in all his arrogance, tie tightened around his neck and draped over a crisp white shirt. A navy blazer sat against matching dress pants and gave way to brown shoes that probably cost more than what Shane had earned at the bar for the entirety of his time there.

The man looked as unfriendly as he was with the hard set of his mouth and the indifference in his eyes. Shane had nothing left to say to him. Shane stepped away from the door, leaving it open. If he wanted to come in, he could do so. It was his property after all.

"I'll be out of here by the end of the week. I know that's what you want."

Grandfather made his way around the couch, finger dragging along the fabric as if he was going to dust check. He quickly shoved his fingers back in his pocket. "That's not what I want."

Shane came to a halt, his head spinning. "It's not?"

"Not at all." He rounded the couch. "Sit."

Shane wanted to defy him, but curiosity had him plopping his ass down.

Grandfather sat on the couch, resting his ankle on his knee. "I need you to understand. I've made a lot of mistakes in my life, but your father was never one of them."

"You have a real shitty way of showing that. First you let him take off and cut you out of his life, then you denied my mother when she came to you for help, and then you've been nothing but a prick to me since I showed up. I never expected you to roll out a red carpet, but I expected a little more hospitality from my own grandfather. I met a lot of people coming here and am grateful for how easily they accepted me into their lives. You have been my biggest disappointment."

Grandfather's brow furrowed, his wrinkles becoming

more defined. "If we're being honest, you've been a big disappointment for me, too."

"That's nice." Shane wasn't going to sit here while they ripped each other down. Shane was more than capable of doing it himself. "I'm sorry if I'm a big disappointment, but you didn't even give me a shot. You avoided me, berated me, and lied to me."

"I know, and I was wrong. I admit that. A part of me is still angry with your father."

"He didn't do anything wrong. You were the one who lied to him."

"I lied to him to give him a better life."

That was the biggest line of bullshit Shane had ever heard. "You lied to him to cover your own ass."

"In the beginning yes, and then after that—" His words faded, realization shining in his eyes.

"You've been holding onto this anger and disappointment with my father all these years, and for what? So you didn't have to face the truth? And now you're taking it out on me. Disappointed in me when there's nothing you know about me to even be disappointed in other than the fact that I'm my father's son."

"No. The reason I'm disappointed is you're leaving."

If Shane's head wasn't attached to his body, it would have whipped around and fell right the hell off. "I thought you'd be happy to get me out of your hair. Happy to get rid of the constant reminder of the son you will always have unfinished business with."

"You really are just like him, you know. Not afraid to

say exactly what's on your mind. But it's one thing to talk a big game. To be a man you have to be willing to back up your words. The moment I met you, I pegged you as a fighter. Then I come here and see that you're ditching town."

"There's nothing left for me here."

"Bullshit!" Grandfather exclaimed, smacking a hand on his leg. "You have family here."

"A family I basically destroyed. Tell me, is Mimi even talking to you?"

"It wouldn't be the first time she's not speaking to me. Your grandmother is much stronger than people give her credit for, and we've weathered worse. But if you're so concerned about supposedly destroying our family, wouldn't a better man stay and fix what he broke?"

"Skipping town is easier for everyone else."

"No. It's easier for him. He'll convince himself that he's doing it for them to justify running."

That's exactly what Shane was doing. He was running—running away from his family, running away from Olivia. If he left them behind, he didn't have to deal with the heartache, pain, and emotions that came with forming relationships and opening his heart to love.

Grandfather rested a hand on Shane's shoulder. It was the first physical contact they'd ever had, and it was surprisingly comforting. "Don't make the same mistake as your father."

Dad had run, just as Shane was doing, and he died never making amends. Shane didn't want that for himself.

He didn't want that for anyone he cared for. "And what about you?"

"I'm here, aren't I?"

chapter 23

It had been less than twenty-four hours since Shane all but shoved Olivia out of his door and out of his life. She was still dumbfounded he had the nerve to text Milo for a ride while they were arguing. Her lip quivered at the memory, but she held back the tears. She cried enough tears for men this month, and she wasn't about to let herself cry any more.

She dropped a few pellets of food into her betta's tank. She still hadn't named him. "What should your name be?" she asked, watching as he sucked in a piece of food. His blue fins fanned out behind him like a majestic king's robe. "How about Sir Phillip?" He fluttered his tail at that exact moment. "I'll take that as a yes. Sir Phillip it is." She tapped the tank, and Sir Phillip followed her finger. "At least you can't leave me. Well, you could die… Don't do that."

Her shift wasn't starting for at least a few hours, and her parents had taken the golf cart to bring John Andre to the beach to run around. Bored, she looked in the fridge, but there was still nothing that she wanted.

She could go for a slice of pie. She just had to avoid the table she and Shane sat at. And the alleyway… the wall… the sidewalk…

She slipped into her sneakers and headed out the door. She didn't even bother looking in the mirror. She had no one to impress. The only person she had to impress was herself. .

Though, she had liked the way Shane's eyes would follow the curve of her bare legs when she was in cute shorts, or how his attention would dip to the low cut of her shirt. The pesky tears stung her eyes, but she forced them back.

He was ridiculous to think that Olivia wouldn't want to be with him. Didn't he realize that a perfectly healthy person could get sick down the road? The future was unpredictable, and his logic was stupid. Not to mention, he took the choice away from her. It shouldn't be his decision if she wanted to be with him; it should be hers.

For a guy who seemed intelligent, well-rounded, and introspective, he was a real dope. She stomped down the driveway, wishing she would have smacked Shane upside the head before she left. Maybe she could have knocked some sense into him.

She was done being disappointed by men. If he didn't want to be with her, she wasn't going to waste another second thinking about him.

She forced every thought of Shane out of her head and continued down the street, focusing her attention on the vibrant flowers lining Ms. Oliver's lawn, the birds chirping in the tall oak tree on the Garrison property, and the two squirrels chasing each other across Harbor Hill Lane.

There was beauty all around her, and she'd ignored it for so long. Living in the city, she was always on the go, walking at rapid speed, going from one place to the next. She never stopped to appreciate anything. Maybe that's why the day she bought her bag became her favorite day. She'd finally allowed herself to slow down and enjoy the moment.

She had no idea where life was going to take her—if she would one day wind up back in the city, or if living in a small town was really where she was meant to be. Either way, she was going to appreciate what she had.

Shane had nothing when he came to Morgan's Bay, but he was content, and Olivia envied that. But the jerk could have more; he could have love if he got beyond his own fears and allowed her in. There was nothing wrong with wanting love.

She groaned to herself. "We're not thinking about him!"

The sound of a car rumbled behind her, and she moved closer to the edge of the road. As the car neared, it slowed. She turned to see who it was, and her smile faltered. Shane looked at her from the driver side, arm hanging out the window, a stupid sparkle in his eyes.

"Need a ride?" he asked.

"Not from you, thank you."

She wasn't going to let him be nice to her after he ended things. She continued walking, but he kept pace beside her. She came to an abrupt halt and about-faced it away from him.

She headed the opposite direction, figuring she could cut down Harbor Hill and take it to Magnolia Drive. A car door slammed shut and she cursed under her breath. She picked up speed. If he wanted to talk then he was going to have to work for it.

He broke her heart, and it would be a snowy day in hell if she was going to lay out the welcome mat for him.

"Olivia, please." His hand touched her elbow, electricity zipping up her arm. She yanked her arm back and stumbled slightly. He reached out, steadying her. Even when she was being a brat, he was still nothing but a gentleman.

She took a deep breath, letting it out slowly. She was furious, and she had every right to be, but if he wanted to talk, then she was willing to listen.

"Please," Shane said, a desperate plea in the brownish green depths of his eyes. "Let me explain."

She crossed her arms over her chest. "I'm listening."

"I'm sorry for last night. You have to know that in my head I was doing it for you. I wanted to protect you from getting hurt."

"You did a real shitty job of it." The pesky tears she'd be holding at bay swelled up and crested against her lids.

He stepped closer to her, and she didn't back up. She let his masculine scent surround her, comfort her. "I'm a coward."

She expected him to say many things, but that was not one of them.

"The minute I realized I was falling in love with you, I panicked."

Her eyes widened at his declaration, heat rushed to her heart, and she could no longer hold back the pesky tears. "You love me?"

He nodded and reached up, dragging a finger down the curve of her face. "I don't want to be your rebound. I want to be your end game."

She wanted to bask in the moment, relish in the glory

of Shane's words, but there was still one problem. "What about all that nonsense about you getting sick? That's why you pushed me away in the first place, is it not?"

"There will always be that possibility that I can get sick again, but I can't live my life in fear, waiting and wondering. What if I never get sick again, and I pushed the best thing that ever happened to me away for nothing? I don't want to live with regrets. The day I die, I want to know that when given the choice, I chose happiness. *You* are my happiness."

She inhaled an ugly breathy snort, warmth spreading through her. "You're mine, too."

"That's good." A smile full of pure joy spread across his face. "My parents fell in love after two weeks together. My mom always said when you know, you know. And I know." Shane's hand slipped into his pocket, and he pulled out his mother's ring.

Olivia's eyes widened at the silver band. "You're not going to propose, are you?"

"Don't look so scared." He laughed.

"I'm not." She wasn't scared. She had only known Shane a short time, but she knew him better than she ever knew Daniel, and Shane knew her, too. And not the girl who tried to be the ideal version of herself, but the girl who made mistakes and wasn't perfect. He had seen her at her very worst, and he'd been at her side ever since.

"Well, I'm not going to propose."

It was too soon, and she thought she'd be relieved, but a touch of sadness came over her.

He cupped her cheek, and she relished in the warmth of

his touch. "I want you to hold onto my mom's ring as a promise that no matter how scary things get, I'll never run."

Her heart burst with joy as he reached into his pocket and pulled out a thin silver chain. "Will you hold onto this for me?"

She nodded, unable to form words. He slid the ring on the chain and stepped behind her. The ring rested against her chest, and she placed her hand over the cool metal. His warm breath stroked her ear, his finger trailing up the delicate skin of her neck.

"I love you," he said.

She spun around and crashed her lips to his, taking the control he so willingly gave her. Her hands thrust into his hair, pulling on the short strands and holding him close. Happiness slammed into her, overwhelming her mind, body, and soul.

It was not so long ago when she had thought she had lost everything, but in losing all the materialistic elements of her life, she was able to find the things that really mattered.

She was able to find true love.

Shane pulled back, pressing a kiss to her nose. He took the ring in his hand and held it up. "And when the time is right, I'll buy you a ring that—"

Her finger rested against his lips. "When the time is right, the only ring I want on my finger is this one."

His lips captured hers hard and fast before he scooped her off her feet and gave her a ride she'd never forget.

Thank you for reading!
Please consider leaving a review.

Preorder your Copy Today

Other Books by Theresa

Mad About Matt

Crushing on Kate

Moments with Mason

Catching Cooper

Hung Up on Hadley

A Bride for Sam

Dreaming of Daisy

Charmed by Chase (Book 1 of the Marshall Family)

Blindsided by Brooke

Lusting After Layla

Jaded Until Jax

Sweet on Sophie (Coming Soon)

<u>Willow Cove</u>
Her Forbidden Love Match
His Not-So Small Town Girl
His Complete Polar Opposite
His Childhood Dream Girl (Coming 2020)

<u>The Again Series</u>
(Never) Again
(Once) Again

<u>Morgan's Bay</u>
All Because of You
All Because I Met You
All Because I Loved You

<u>Written with Cassie Mae under the pen name Tessa Marie</u>
Broken Records

Become a Townie

A group for readers of Theresa Paolo's books. A place to get to know the writer behind the screen and also to receive all the up-to-date information on sales, new releases, cover reveals, and to discuss her books. Becoming a Townie also gives you access to exclusive content and giveaways.

Join today by clicking here.

Acknowledgements

To my readers, you are the reason I get to continue to do what it is that I love so much. Your support means the world to me, and has kept me going even on those days when the words aren't flowing and I want to give up. Thank you from the bottom of my heart for continuing to show up and support me.

Cassie after all these books I'm running out of ways to tell you that you're awesome and I couldn't do this without you. Thanks for giving me your ear when I need to work something out and your voice when I can't seem to see reason. Thanks for not throwing your computer out the window when you lost thirty pages of notes… You're the bestest!

Mom, there are so many pieces to the puzzle in getting a book from idea to finish draft and you are a big piece of that puzzle. Without you, my books wouldn't be the same. Thank you for reading chapter after chapter, draft after draft and always offering your honest unbiased opinion even if it's hard for me to hear.

Beta Girls, thanks for your friendship and your support from the very beginning. I love you girls!

Eric thank you for bringing me home Cadbury Mini and Crème eggs, cooking dinner when I just don't have it in me and for loving me even when I haven't showered in two days, my hair is a mess and I'm wearing the same pair of yoga pants.

Amanda, thanks for this awesome cover. You captured exactly what I wanted for this series.

To the TV show *Turn*, thank you for a much needed distraction when my brain was desperate for a break.

About the Author

Theresa Paolo lives on Long Island, NY with her fiancé and their fish. She is the author of NA and Adult contemporary romances. Her debut novel (NEVER) AGAIN, released in Fall 2013 with Berkley (Penguin) and the companion novel (ONCE) AGAIN released Summer 2014. Mad About Matt, the first book in her new Red Maple Falls series, released March 2017.

She loves to write heartfelt romances with a dash of fun and a side of spice. When she's not writing, she's reading, brewery hopping, daydreaming, wasting time on Pinterest, or can be found chatting away on Twitter and Facebook.

She writes YA romance under Tessa Marie.

www.ingramcontent.com/pod-product-compliance
Lightning Source LLC
Chambersburg PA
CBHW051222130726
47988CB00001B/192